# THE YOUNG PRETENDERS

Persephone Book Nº73
Published by Persephone Books Ltd 2007

First published by Longmans, Green & Co, 1895

Preface © Charlotte Mitchell 2007

The endpaper is taken from 'Apple'
designed by Lindsay P Butterfield for
GP & J Baker c. 1895
© V&A Images/Victoria and Albert Museum

Typeset in ITC Baskerville by Keystroke,
High Street, Tettenhall, Wolverhampton

Colour by Banbury Litho

Printed and bound by Biddles Ltd, King's Lynn

ISBN  978 1 903155 639

Persephone Books Ltd
59 Lamb's Conduit Street
London WC1N 3NB
020 7242 9292

www.persephonebooks.co.uk

THE YOUNG PRETENDERS

*by*

EDITH HENRIETTA FOWLER

\*\*\*\*\*\*\*

*with illustrations by*

PHILIP BURNE-JONES

*and a new preface by*

CHARLOTTE MITCHELL

PERSEPHONE BOOKS
LONDON

# PREFACE

**✳✳✳✳✳✳✳**

I was brought up with this book but its delightful qualities are known to few people. First published in 1895, reprinted in 1911 and never since, it is the story of two children (or really of one child, Babs Conway, because her elder brother is quite uninteresting to anyone except her). They belong to a group of children who in their generation and class were fairly numerous: those sent Home from India, or elsewhere in the East, by parents serving the Empire, to grow up in the charge of more or less affectionate relations or guardians.

Few living people remember this predicament, but it was immortalised in Kipling's 'Baa Baa Black Sheep' (1888), a story written from bitter personal experience and still-burning rancour. One could add to the list of work inspired in this way Saki's 'Sredni Vashtar' (1911) and 'The Lumber-Room' (1914), which draw on his own sufferings at the hands of his ghastly aunts, and also much of the aunt-related fiction of PG Wodehouse.

*The Young Pretenders*, though it is heart-rending at moments, and certainly deplores the necessity of dividing children from their parents, is much more cheerful than Kipling's story. Unlike these writers, its author was not remembering her own childhood, for although her father, a solicitor and Liberal politician, was Secretary of State for India in 1894–5, he never seems to have visited it, and all the evidence suggests that hers was a particularly close and affectionate family.

Edith Henrietta Fowler was the younger of the two writing daughters of Henry Hartley Fowler (1830-1911), who was born in Wolverhampton, the clever and determined son of a Methodist minister. By hard work and good luck he achieved immense success, rising to prominence in the Liberal party, serving for many years as a cabinet minister and being first knighted and then ennobled as Viscount Wolverhampton, the first Methodist to be raised to the peerage, and the first Methodist and the first solicitor to enter the cabinet. Queen Victoria was particularly fond of Sir Henry Fowler: the courtier Sir Frederick Ponsonby recorded cattily in his memoirs that this was because he 'agreed with all the Queen said'. He was sufficiently important that he still figures prominently in the history of late-Victorian Liberalism. (More details of his story, with photographs and material of interest to local historians, have been gathered by Anthony Perry in *The Fowler Legacy: The Story of a Forgotten Family*, 1997.)

The special flavour of the Fowler sisters' fiction derives from the fact that they knew well both the life of the professional middle-classes in the provinces and the still largely aristocratic circles of late Victorian and Edwardian government. Although they never let you forget that they were thoroughly at home in high society, and although they, unlike their father, were brought up as members of the Church of England, they also felt loyalty to his middle-class nonconformist family traditions, and gently satirised upper-class pretension and worldliness. A particularly engaging picture of the home life of mid-Victorian dissenting clergy is given in *Concerning Isabel Carnaby* (1898), the work for which Edith's elder sister Ellen Thorneycroft Fowler was best known.

There is a decided family resemblance between the adult fiction of the two sisters: both wrote witty society novels with strong religious themes and plenty of epigrammatic dialogue, in which sparky girls fall in love with strong, silent, serious and high-minded men. Ellen was much the more prolific and the more successful; she also published verse. Neither sister married until 1903, having had what Edith calls in one of her books an 'overgrown girlhood' in their parents' house, where they no doubt played their parts in the elaborate public social life of a politician in the age of empire.

Edith was a childless spinster of thirty when she published her first book, *The Young Pretenders*, which was followed by another children's book two years later. She also contributed stories of child-life to *Longman's Magazine*, and perhaps to other periodicals, in the 1890s. Two novels for adults followed in 1899 and 1901 before her marriage in 1903 (at the fairly advanced age of thirty-eight) to the Rev. Robert Hamilton (1868–1954), successively vicar of St. George's, Wolverhampton (1896–1902), Sutton Bonington, near Loughborough (1902–1920), and East Malling, Kent (1920-1934), who was decorated for service as a chaplain with the Italian army in 1918–1920. Their two sons were born in 1905 and 1908.

During her marriage she published three more novels at long intervals, in 1905, 1915 and 1921. She also wrote a workmanlike, informative and devoted, but slightly dull, biography of her father in 1912. Though her novel *Patricia* (1915), in which a brilliant rather bohemian girl is tamed by a clergyman peer, is well worth reading, her best work is in the first two books, which paint a singularly vivid picture of the pleasures and pains of late Victorian upper middle-class childhood.

*The Young Pretenders* is written from a child's point of view and all the villains are grown-ups. Like many Victorian children's books it reminds its readers of the moral dangers of thoughtlessness and selfishness, but its targets are the casual crimes committed by adults against children. There is a wonderful moment when the children are playing happily on the beach with their beloved uncle who starts making them a sandcastle. Then he gets bored: '"That's the worst of grown-ups,' said Teddy, 'they get tired of things so quick."'

On another occasion they invade his study and he is charming; next day they go back again but he is in a bad temper and takes it out on them. The reader is made to feel all the incredible unfairness of this, and also what a normal feature of child experience this kind of inexplicable inconsistency is. But this is to make the book sound solemn and portentous when its great characteristic is a gay malicious irony. Much of its charm comes from its account of the way children think, the way they talk and their unarticulated misunderstandings of the adult world. Consols, the government stocks whose fall makes their uncle anxious for his private income, get muddled up in their heads with the Roman

**\*\*\*\*\*\*\*\*\*\***

consuls of their dreary history lessons: 'Big old Mr Consol has glaring eyes and black whiskers, and great teeth, and one day he went out to find a good person to eat . . .'

As anyone who has tried to bring up children knows, you spend a good deal of time teaching them to be insincere, to simulate gratitude or contrition, and not to repeat other people's comments at the wrong moment. Many of Fowler's jokes depend on the fact that Babs has yet to learn these lessons. 'Giles always said Uncle Charley had married one as would be more for ornament than use', she says to beautiful, selfish Aunt Eleanor. And to the horrible governess:

> 'Uncle Charley didn't fink it at all naughty to call you a beast... he seemed rather glad,' Teddy said. 'P'r'aps he and Aunt Eleanor don't fink beast a rude name. I don't 'spect they can, 'cause Aunt Eleanor said you were a cat, and in course she couldn't be rude. But a cat is a beast too, isn't it?'

Really to enjoy this book, you have to relish these jokes about the things children say. 'I don't yike bacon in my cake', said by a little boy rejecting a piece of candied peel in Edith Fowler's second book, *The Professor's Children*, has become a catchphrase in my family. There was definitely a fashion for baby talk in late Victorian children's books, and not all of it appeals to the modern reader. The heroine of Stella Austin's *Stumps* (1873) is apt to say, ''Tumps is derry derry sorry' rather too often, and the hero of Mary Louisa Molesworth's *The Adventures of Herr Baby* (1881) to talk about himself in the third person, 'Him is so sorry, so werry sorry'. The novelist Charlotte M Yonge, who edited a magazine for girls to which Mrs Molesworth contributed, asked her whether she really thought children found 'phonetic spellings of their lispings' easy to read. Probably she also meant that it had become an affectation in some writers, and certainly it must have been adults rather than children who thought it sweet.

Children's books are of course normally bought by adults, and are often read by adults to children: the inclusion of jokes and references incomprehensible to children is nothing unusual in their history. All the same, the baby talk trend probably reflects the existence of a market for books about children partly aimed at an adult readership, to which *The Young Pretenders*, and also *The Professor's Children,* belong.

Semi-autobiographical works such as Kenneth Grahame's *Dream Days* (1899) and Lizzie Harker's *A Romance of the Nursery* (1902) also fall into this class. The mother who read these books, either aloud or to herself, was being offered ideas on how to bring up children, gentle comedy of child-life and an enjoyable and undemanding read. Both Fowler's children's books show signs of being influenced by contemporary debate about the ideas of such educationists as Friedrich Fröbel and Maria Montessori, which are there opposed to old-fashioned rote-learning. Babs's only positive educational experience in London comes from a governess who lets her model animals in clay, which was one of the techniques encouraged in the Fröbel system. *The Professor's Children* is about the unfortunate motherless offspring of a professor of child psychology, who are shut up in a dull house in Bloomsbury (he probably worked in my own college, University College London, which pioneered the study of child psychology in Britain, though he never seems to see any students) and made to learn German so they will be able to read scientific textbooks. Like Babs and Teddy Conway, they alleviate their grim existence by developing a rich fantasy life. By the end, luckily, the professor sees the light and takes them to live an outdoor life by the seaside, playing with animals and learning from direct experience.

The engaging illustrations in *The Young Pretenders* are by Philip Burne-Jones (1861–1926), the son of the painter and first cousin to Rudyard Kipling (for whom occasional visits to his Burne-Jones aunt and uncle were among the few pleasures of his miserable childhood exile). The Fowlers and Burne-Jones had long been acquainted because Philip's grandfather, the Rev George Macdonald, had been minister of the Methodist church in Wolverhampton attended by Henry Fowler, and when Edith wrote a biography of her father another Macdonald sister, Louisa Baldwin, contributed affectionate memories of the elder Fowler family's kindness to her when she was young.

Burne-Jones was an artist who never equalled his father's professional success and illustrated only a handful of other books. His work here is a reminder of the sentimental delight taken by many Victorians in picturesque children, something which Fowler herself satirises in this book. As she points out, such feelings are quite distinct from enjoying the company of children, and from being able to sympathise with them and make them happy. This opposition between real affection for

**\*\*\*\*\*\*\*\*\*\***

children and artificial feeling about them is in fact her central theme:

> 'Oh, I do wish she had been a doll! I've told such a lot of people about the little niece that I'm going to have, and now I shall be ashamed to show her, from what you say . . . If she'd been like Barbara now, I would have taken her about with me, and it would have been fun to have dressed her. I like the look of a pretty little girl in a victoria.'

This is the loathsome Aunt Eleanor speaking. It is left to the reader's imagination what her punishment will be, though it is apparent by the end of the book that Babs's visit has created a terminal rift in a hitherto perfectly satisfactory marriage, and by implication we are reassured that thus all enemies and oppressors of vulnerable children will be gloriously defeated.

Charlotte Mitchell
London, 2007

# THE YOUNG PRETENDERS

IN THE GARDEN.

# CONTENTS.

# ILLUSTRATIONS.

# THE YOUNG PRETENDERS.

## CHAPTER I.

### IN THE GARDEN.

GRANNIE would never come back any more. At least that was what nurse said, and so the children knew that it must be true.

"When we're grown up shall we know everything right like Nana does?" asked Babs, as they talked it over afterwards in the garden.

"I daresay," answered Teddy carelessly. "What shall we play at now, Babs?" So the children forgot the news that nurse had told them, and cheerfully accepted the fact that their grandmother, with whom they had lived during the whole of their short lives, had gone away indeed beyond recall. It did not matter much to them. They had always thought of Grannie as a piece of the drawing-room furniture, quite a nice piece, but dull and delicate as most drawing-room furni-

ture is to the child mind. She had never
entered into their world at all. That was
peopled by a host of pretending folk, all the
animals they ever came across, and most of the
servants with their relatives and acquaintances
inclusive. Such an interesting world it was,
bounded by the brook and the lanes, and full
of excitement in the first bird's nest, and the
young rabbits, to say nothing of Giles the
gardener's thrilling stories!

And besides it was several weeks now since
Grannie had gone away to London, and the
memory of her was already growing a little
dim. Teddy and Babs had both almost cried
their eyes out when Don the retriever died;
—but then he was a real friend of theirs, and
that makes a great difference.

"Good-morning, little master and missy!"
said Giles, as the two children peeped in at the
tool-house door. "Has nurse told you the
sad news?"

"No, what?" cried Babs anxiously. "Soot
hasn't been caught in a trap again, has she?"
And the little girl's face paled with appre-
hension.

"I mean about your poor, dear grandma."

"Oh, is that all?" said Babs with a sigh of

relief. "You gived me such a fright 'bout darling Soot!"

"Nana told us Grannie isn't never coming home again," answered Teddy; "but, Giles, do take us to see the nest you found yesterday."

"Yes, do!" pleaded Babs.

"Sakes alive!" ejaculated the old man, "what callous creatures children be," and he drew his horny hand across his eyes and finished the plant he was potting before they all three started for the plantation, the children dancing round him with the delight of a couple of terriers just turned out of the kennel.

"Teddy," said Babs, when their excitement about the nest had abated, and the gardener gone back to his work, "if that other big nest right up at the top of the tree that Giles told us 'bout, is so high what no ladders can reach it, how did anybody reach to put the eggs in?"

This was rather a poser for Teddy. But that was the worst of Babs. She was always asking such difficult questions, and Teddy deep down in his masculine mind could not bear to own that he did not know.

"I 'spect somebody climbed," he said dubiously.

"Oh, who?" asked his sister eagerly. "It

couldn't have been Giles, nor Nana, nor Grannie, nor the gardener's boy, 'cause I asked him
specially if he couldn't get me one of the eggs
for our c'lection, and he said it was much too
high.   Who could it be ? "

" Somebody in the night ; p'r'aps a fairy."

" P'r'aps an angel.   Oh, yes," surmised Babs,
" that must be it.   One of those I 'spect out of
' Four corners to my bed '."

" Yes," said Teddy, thankful that the subject
was satisfactorily settled, " on their way down,
you know."

" What shall we play at, now ? " continued
the little girl.   " Let's pretend we're the
Stoners."

Mr. and Mrs. Stoner were a very erratic
couple, whose varied experiences were Babs's
great delight.   She was always Mrs. Stoner—
the fond mother of a most dilapidated family
of dolls, and a cheery, chatty matron, notwithstanding all her cares, and Teddy was Mr.
Stoner.   At least he always began by being
Mr. Stoner, and then to Babs's sorrow he generally turned out to be either a prince in disguise,
or a terrifyingly wicked man called Henry
Baker.   It was naturally very upsetting for Mrs.
Stoner when either of these changes took place,

and, indeed, on one memorable occasion her husband had suddenly become a lion, which was manifestly perturbing in any well-regulated household. Poor Babs used to implore Teddy not to turn out into anybody else. But he was rather a romantic boy and enjoyed the unexpected. Moreover, he had one great advantage over Babs which influenced his style of play; he, being seven years old, could read exciting fairy tales and work out his pretences on those lines; while his little sister, being only five, was out of all this. For such sentences as " that fat cat," which were at present her literary boundaries, did not tend to inspire fresh thoughts or ideals.

" Don't turn out to be any one else," pleaded Babs, " be just Mr. Stoner."

" I can't be sure," said Teddy solemnly.

" Well, then, do begin by being the prince. I'd rather have that than turning out."

But in the end, as usual, Babs played Teddy's way, and Mrs. Stoner opened proceedings by giving a sumptuous dinner-party. Her only guests were snap-dragons, chosen as most suitable for banquets on account of their swallowing capabilities. It was such fun poking down their open throats with a bit of stick, first some chopped grass out of the mower's wheelbarrow, mixed with water, and then a soil pudding made from the hostess's own receipt.

"What shall we do now their froats is full?" asked Babs anxiously before the last course.

"I'll be the doctor," said Teddy.

"Do people ever have the doctor right in the middle of the dinner-party?"

"They might, if they were very ill."

Rap, rap, rap, on the trunk of the tree, and Mrs. Stoner flushed and excited admitted Doctor Teddy. Oh, then they had a lovely time, peering into the snap-dragons' throats, and pouring water down, and, in extreme cases, extracting the tongues from the back of the flower.

"It's just like us when we had sore froats," cried Babs excitedly.

By the time the doctoring was done, some of the snap-dragons were very languid and weak.

"They don't open their mouths kite so nice," said anxious Mrs. Stoner, stroking them tenderly with her fat brown fingers.

"They're very bad still," pronounced the doctor gravely.

"An' this dear white one is all split."

" Then it must be drowned," continued the medical man, whose measures were drastic.

" Oh, Teddy," gasped the little girl sympathetically, " must it really ? "

" Yes ; we will go down to the brook with it now."

So the tender little hostess bowed to the doctor's stern decree, and they set out across the field towards the brook with fatal purpose.

" Let me kiss it afore it goes," asked Babs, as they stood on the bridge.   And then, after sad farewells, they solemnly dropped the ragged flower into the water.

A moment's mournful silence ensued.

" Let's paddle," suggested Teddy, chiefly to cheer Babs's drooping spirits at the snapdragon's decease.

The thought of wading in the cool water on that hot morning filled the little girl with a sudden reaction of delight.   They tore off their shoes and stockings, and ran about on the fresh grass before venturing into the brook.

" I'se still Mrs. Stoner," said Babs.

" I'm Henry Baker," announced Teddy.

The worst had happened, for there was nothing which filled poor Babs with greater terror than these sudden appearances of Henry Baker.

"Oh, please not, Teddy," she gasped. "Be a prince instead!"

"Henry Baker is a wicked man," said Teddy, utterly unmoved by her appeal; "he cut all his children up in slices."

The horror of this announcement was too much for Babs. In her hurry to reach dry land, she dropped her little bunch of petti-coats and frock, trod on a sharp stone, and finally fell down in the soft red mud that lined the banks of the brook.

"What a mess!" observed Teddy unsym-pathetically.

Babs looked extremely surprised for a few moments, and then, as if to complete the catas-trophe, she began to splash violently with both hands.

"You'd better come out," continued Teddy, as his sister sat resignedly in water several inches deep; and then from a scientific point of view : "What does it feel like, Babs?"

"Rather cold in the water and warmish in the mud," catching her breath.

"Anything like hasty pudding would be?"

" Yes, something.   On'y kite cold hasty pudding."

" More like porridge, perhaps ? "

" Oh, yes," cried Babs, cheering up, " just
like porridge and lots of cold milk."

" You'd better go in," repeated Teddy,
" 'cause of catching cold."

" It's a horrid feeling," said Babs, as she
scrambled up, " all heavy and dripping."

" It's horrider catching cold and stopping all
day in bed," observed Teddy wisely ; and his
little sister took the hint and started to run
towards the house as fast as she could in her
wet, clinging clothes.

Nana was a lovely nurse to go to in a mess.
She never scolded at all, but put Babs into a
nice warm bath, and dressed her in clean, dry
things, only muttering to herself every now and
then, " Poor lambs ! gone to-day, and here
again to-morrow," which remark Babs did not
understand at all, and that cannot be wondered
at, for to whom could it possibly apply ?   The
children were not gone to-day, and Grannie,
who was, would not be here again to-morrow ;
or indeed, as Nana had said, ever again.   Still
it seemed to relieve nurse's feelings, and that
was the principal thing.   One of the under-

maids had ventured to laugh at this saying of
Nana's that same morning, but had been sternly
rebuked for making jokes when death was in
the house.

" It ain't in the 'ouse any way," she rudely
retorted.

" It's in the Family, and that's the same
thing," said nurse with dignity, as she left the
room.   Nana always spelt the family with a
capital F.

" Now, Miss Babs, dear," when the toilet
was completed, " you'd better not go out again
just at present, wait till after dinner, there's a
love."

Ordinarily this prohibition would have raised
a storm, but the little girl astonished nurse by
saying, " All right," as she ran off into the day
nursery.

" It's as if the dear lamb's thoughts were in
Heaven, too," said Nana, wiping away a tear.

But she was mistaken.   The dear lamb was
thinking solely of some very interesting birds'
eggs which she and Teddy were trying to hatch
on the top of the hot water cistern.   And for
some time she had been trying to persuade him
to let her make a hole in one of them with a
pin, just to see how they were getting on, but

in vain. This seemed a golden opportunity, for the children were nearly always together. So Babs started off to the attics, armed with a large pin to aid her research.

" The eggs is addled, Teddy," she announced at dinner.

" How do you know ? " asked her brother sharply.

" I made just a teeny, weeny hole in one with a pin, and I couldn't see nothing."

" You'd no business to," said Teddy crossly. " Now you've spoilt that one. I told you not."

" Oh, Teddy, I haven't killed the little bird ? " she asked in an agony.

" Yes ; you have."

Here nurse had to interfere, as Babs was almost in tears, and Teddy quite in a temper.

" If there's any quarrelling about it I shall have to throw the whole lot away," she threatened ; and the children were drawn together again by the bond of a common danger to their beloved property.

Four years ago Major and Mrs. Conway went back to India leaving their two children to live in the dear old country home with Grannie. She did not know much about children, poor old lady, or perhaps she had forgotten what she once knew. It was so long since the major and his younger brother were little boys in the Cloverdale nursery, and that dear, dead daughter of hers a baby girl. And besides she had latterly become a regular invalid, and could not do with the noise of childish voices and rough games.

So Teddy and Babs had lived alone, going their own way and working out their own thoughts. Nana was very good in caring for their creature comforts, but she was rather old and fumbling too, and they had never known the joy of an under-nurse ; one of those scatter-brained, jovial village girls who work so badly and play so splendidly. So the children's chief and only playfellow had been the gardener Giles.

All day, every day, unless the weather was too bad, they spent out of doors, playing their quaint games and pretences, and growing with the birds and flowers in Nature's big nursery, quite independently of the training and teaching which children usually have. A happy, sunshiny life it was, and Cloverdale, the best, biggest, home-country in the world.

But with just the same surroundings the two children were entirely different—different in

looks and ways and character. And it seemed
as if there were a mistake somewhere—that
Teddy should have been the girl and Babs the
boy. For Teddy had a sweet, fair face, framed
in golden hair, his lovely mother's face, in fact,
that ought to have been her daughter's. And
Babs, poor Babs! was dark and square and
sunburnt. A plain, cheerful child, full of the
tenderest sensibilities, consumed by the most
ardent feelings. While Teddy smiled an angel
smile and did not care much really about anything.

" I will conjure this afternoon," announced
the little boy magnanimously, and Babs's delighted excitement knew no bounds. The conjuring pigs were quite an institution in the
Cloverdale nursery. They originally came out
of a Noah's ark, which Grannie had given
Teddy one far-away Christmas, and consequently were both exactly alike.

" Where will you conjure to ? " asked Babs
with the deepest interest.

" I will conjure this one into the wheelbarrow
on the lawn, hidden in the grass," said Teddy,
with a lordly air. " Look, here it is in my
hand. You see it, and touch it ? "

" Yes," exclaimed his little sister in an awe-stricken manner at the approach of so great a mystery.

"Well, look here! Be gone, pig! One, two, three, and away," and he waved his closed hand wildly in the air. "Now, Babs, go to the wheelbarrow and see if it's there."

Away flew little Barbara downstairs and out at the garden door. She buried both her fat hands in the mown grass, and sure enough there lay a little wooden pig.

"Oh, Teddy!" she screamed, "here it is. How wonderful you conjure! How do you do it?"

But her brother never would tell. He enjoyed her wondering admiration of his skill, and proceeded to electrify her still further by conjuring the pig back into the nursery cupboard.

"Again," she implored. "I'se thought of a place this time—into the rabbit-hutch."

But Teddy said the conjuring was over for that day, and Babs could not persuade him further. So they took all the young rabbits out in the orchard and played with them happily till tea-time, when Nana arrived with the joyful announcement that they might have tea in the little tea-things on the lawn.

A slight squabble arose as to who should
pour out, which was decided by a compromise
suggested by nurse.   Babs should help the
milk and sugar and Teddy pour the tea.   Tea
in the little tea-things always ended with a
delightful game called "lappety," which consisted of a race between the children as to
who could first drink a whole cup of milk,
spooning it up with one of the tiny tea-spoons.
It was very exciting, as Babs in her hurry
generally choked, and then Teddy got so far
ahead that he was sure to win.   On this occasion it ended more roughly still, the teapot was
upset and the tray swam with a miscellany of
slops, which fluid Teddy finally insisted that
Babs should drink.   The little girl obediently
complied.   She was accustomed from earliest
youth to drink the leavings of a little tea-things
party, and had apparently quite acquired the
taste.

" Uncle Charley's coming to see us soon,"
said Teddy ; "Giles told me."

" Oh, how lovely ! " cried Babs.   " We haven't
never seen him all our lives, have we ? "

" Of course not ; he's been in India as well
as Father, but he came home when Grannie
went to London."

"He'll be splendid, won't he, Teddy? A real Inja soldier!"

A very favourite game of the children's was pretending to be Father and Uncle Charley.

"I'm awful glad he's really coming," continued the boy, "'cause he's been in a proper battle, you know, Babs. Giles told me all about it; and got a medal from the Queen 'cause of it."

"Oh, yes; I know. Giles tells us lovely tales 'bout Uncle Charley."

"I shall be a soldier too, Babs, of course."

"Of course. But, Teddy, I wish Father had been in a battle, too. It makes it so much more of a soldier."

"He might have got killed," suggested Teddy.

"Oh! so he might. I'm awful glad now it was Uncle Charley as was in the battle."

"And I am. His medal'll look lovely on his scarlet coat. Won't it, Babs?"

"Oh, lovely! When's he coming? I'm so 'cited 'bout it."

"One day quite soon, Giles says."

"Master Teddy, Master Teddy!" called Nana from the window; "I want you."

The children rushed in and found nurse

poring over a little thin piece of pink paper
which had come in an orange envelope.

" I'm to take you up to London to-morrow,
Master Teddy, dear, your uncle says."

" What does it say?" asked Teddy, who
could not quite manage to read writing yet.

" Bring the boy here to-morrow for funeral,
by eleven train to Paddington. Will meet you.
—Captain Conway."

" Not me too?" cried Babs, with a dawning
fear.

" No, dearie," said Nana lovingly, " but
we'll only be gone a day or two."

" Oh, I would so have 'joyed the funeral!"
cried Babs, " why didn't they want me too?"

" There, there, miss dearie, don't fret.
Funerals aren't nice for little girls;" which
sounded as if nurse thought them delightful for
every one else.

" I wish I was going, too," continued Babs,
wailing.

But Nana came to the rescue with kisses of
comfort, and suggested that the little girl should
sail boats during her bath; and this was a stroke
of genius on the part of nurse.

Babs's distress vanished as if by magic, and
judging from the shouts of laughter and splash-

ing which emerged from the bathroom during her ablutions, the trouble was apparently quite forgotten.   For happily children's sorrows, though perhaps as keen as those of their elders, are nothing like so long-lived.

Teddy was not nearly so excitable as his little sister, and took the news of his coming journey very calmly.   He methodically set about packing his best top and paint-box in case he wanted either of them at the funeral.   And nurse attended to such details as clothes after the children were safe in bed.

They both sat up till nearly eight o'clock on this memorable occasion, and Babs was spared the anguish of that half-hour which usually came after her bed-time and before her brother's.

" Teddy," she called, the last thing, just before Nana shut the night nursery door, " s'pose the eggs hatch while you're away, what must I give them to eat ? "

" Bread and milk," said Teddy.

" And just a few worms mixed with it ?  You remember how our last starling but one 'joyed bread and milk and worms ? "

" Now, children, no more talking, or I shall have to shut Master Teddy's bedroom door."

" I'se rather glad after all that I'll be at home

in case those eggs do hatch," murmured Babs to herself. " It would be so lonesome for the little ones without me for their mother."

And the dear little mother-soul within her rejoiced that no pleasure of hers should interfere with her loving maternal duties. Which is the way of mothers.

## CHAPTER II.

### UNCLE CHARLEY.

BUT Teddy and Nana did not come back again soon. Four, five long summer days went by, and Babs was still alone at Cloverdale.

She was enjoying herself immensely. It was such a treat going down to tea in the servants' hall, such fun helping Giles all day to garden, and listening to his thrilling conversation. Uncle Charley was the never-failing theme. Giles waxed so eloquent on the heroic conduct of British soldiers, and Babs caught his spirit and tone in a manner which even indulgent Nana would have noticed and rebuked.

At last a letter came to cook, telling her to prepare for Captain Conway, who was coming down to Cloverdale that very night.

It was very tiresome that he would not arrive till long after Babs was asleep, but on the following morning, directly she knew that he had gone downstairs, she rushed into the dining-

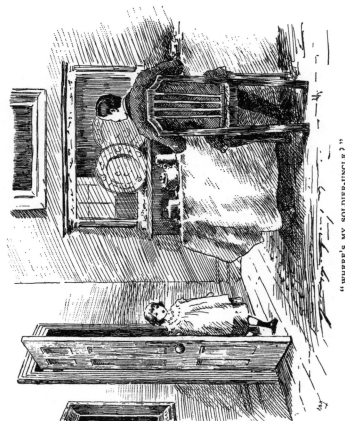

"WHERE'S MY SOLDIER-UNCLE?"

room in ecstatic anticipation of her introduction
to this heroic soldier-uncle.

A slight, fair young man sat at the table,
pouring out a cup of tea.

"Where's my soldier-uncle?" asked Babs,
aghast, with an anxious little quaver in her
voice. "I want to see him."

"Good gracious! is that really the girl?"
thought Captain Conway, as he looked at the
sturdy, brown little maiden before him, and
looked in vain for some likeness to that lovely,
stately woman who was his brother's wife.

"I want my Uncle Charley!" she repeated
impatiently; "you can go away, strange man."

"But look here, child, I am your Uncle
Charley. Don't you know me?"

How could she have known him when he had
been in India for the whole five years of her
short life? But he could not think of anything
else to say. This first appearance of his niece
had so greatly disconcerted him. The boy
was so pretty and graceful and taking that
both his uncle and aunt were delighted with
him. And Captain Conway had vaguely expected that when he went to Cloverdale a trim-
looking maid would have brought to him a well-
dressed, golden-haired, fairy kind of child, who

would have kissed him prettily, and lisped out some polite, orthodox greeting ; instead of which the door had been flung open, and, transfixed at the sight of him, a square, brown, plain, untidy little creature had stood on the threshold, impatiently demanding that he should go away, and that her Uncle Charley should come.

" I am your Uncle Charley." Then as if to himself : " Imagine this being Barbara's child ! "

To his great surprise the little girl stamped her foot in a sudden frenzy of passion.

" Go away, nasty strange man," she repeated. " They told me my uncle was a soldier, and I'se not a Barbara child. They calls me Babs."

" It is all right, I am a soldier," he said soothingly, " and I have come all this long way from London to see you."

" I thought you'd be 'zackly like this," she explained, drawing nearer, and the smart young officer looked with amazement on a hideous advertisement for recruits, which portrayed a red-cheeked soldier blowing a trumpet ; " and Giles always says as the British soldier is the pride o' the nation, and I was so glad my uncle was one, and now you are quite different, not a bit like the pride o' the nation, and no sword nor medal nor nothing," and she looked at him reproachfully.

"Never mind about that," exclaimed her uncle; "I'm not dressed like a soldier to-day. I've got lots of scarlet coats and swords in London, and you shall see them all if you will be good."

Babs's face brightened at this cheering news.

"And a trumpet and shield?" she asked eagerly.

"Yes, yes, everything," answered the captain, with a slight disregard of the truth, and in the hope of diverting her. "Who is Giles?"

"I love Giles," said Babs, forgetting her disappointment; "he is Teddy's and my best friend next to Nana. You see Grannie was gener'ly ill. Giles said she'd got the chronic, and since Teddy and Nana went to London I've lived in the garden, and goin' about with Giles more'n ever, and we've had the loveliest talks 'bout you, and the crops, and when the old pig'll be ready for killing; and I weed, and dig, and help Giles all day. Let me go now," continued the child, pulling away from his hand, "I shall just catch him while he's feedin' the fowls!"

"So that is the girl," thought the captain, a vexed look sweeping over his face. "What a pity! But this running wild and being the companion of some farm-labourer must be put a stop to. It is most unfortunate. She is not a bit like a gentleman's child, either to look at or to talk to. Fat brown legs, covered with scratches, filthy hands, hair that looks as if it had never been brushed or cut, frock fit for the workhouse, accent atrocious, manners and education entirely lacking."

So the fastidious, dandified captain reckoned up his small niece's enormities, and resolved that things should be very differently managed now the children were under his control.

For Captain and Mrs. Conway had decided to take Teddy and Babs home with them to London, and keep them until their parents came back from India, to settle in the old home at Cloverdale.

"I've 'splained to Giles about your being not a bit like a soldier to look at," said Babs, on her return to the room a few minutes later, "an' he says as elders and betters must be honoured in spite o' their looks, which, as they didn't make themselves, is no fault of theirn."

"Babs!" exclaimed her uncle; "you really

must not talk like that, it's not at all like a little lady."

The brown eyes filled with tears, and an ominous pucker round the mouth caused Captain Conway to add hurriedly : "There, there, don't cry! Here's a new shilling for you."

Babs brightened up in a moment, and took the peace-offering with delight.

"I've never had so much money in my life afore," she said excitedly, "I never have nothing but pennies, 'cept the threepenny bits on Sunday, which Giles says take as natural to the off'tory bags as ducklings do to duck-ponds."

Captain Conway sighed, but Babs went on cheerfully : "I'd like to see you in your scarlet coat soon, with your spear and shield. Do you often kill people now, Uncle Charley?"

"No, not often," laughed the young man.

"On'y wicked people, I s'pose?"

"Not anybody at all."

Babs looked woefully disappointed, until a fresh thought suddenly diverted her : "May I crack your egg for you? Do let me, I can do it so nice."

As her uncle was afraid of vexing her again, he resignedly acquiesced.

"There's always the chance of finding a

chicken in it, you see," she continued, "that's what makes eggs so interesting for breakfast. We only have them on Sundays, so we on'y get very few chances."

"Have you got any real chickens out of doors?"

"Oh, yes; splendid ones. All the bantams are mine, and the others Teddy's."

"I'm afraid you are very fond of the country," said her uncle, trying to picture this wild, out-of-door child shut up in a London nursery.

"What are you 'fraid of in the country?" she asked. "The cows? I'm not a bit 'fraid of them, an' I milk the dear, white one sometimes when Giles holds her tail. I can't bear it to come whiskin' round."

"And have you got any dogs or cats?"

"Why, of course we have! I love Soot, the cat, better than any one in the whole world, 'cept Teddy and Nana, and Giles, and Father-and-Mother-in-Inja. She hasn't had any more kittens lately. It seems a longer time than gener'ly is since she had any. Poor thing! her kittens hardly ever live to grow up, but Giles says that cats have a sight o' trouble in that way."

"And what dogs?"

" Oh ! Sheepie, and Toby, and Dash. Dear
Don died last week, or p'r'aps it was last year ;
I forget. Mrs. Forrester gived us Toby."

" Who is Mrs. Forrester ? "

" Don't you know ? Why, Jane's aunt—the
laundry-maid, you know—she lives in the village, and her niece, 'Lizabeth Lamb, lives with
her, who has got the decline. Mrs. Forrester
gived a party the day after Nana and Teddy
went to London, and I went and Jane and
Giles. I did 'joy myself. Giles wore his Sunday coat, and Mrs. Forrester on'y cried twice."

" Does Mrs. Forrester often cry ? " asked the
captain, who could not help being amused by
this torrent of talk.

" Oh, gener'ly ! You know she has to every
time she sees Mr. Forrester's funeral card,
what's framed, and you can't help seeing it
pretty often 'cause of its being over the chimney-
piece. It gives her a turn, she always says,
but Giles finks her res'voirs leak."

Then seeing him put his cup down, she
added hurriedly :—

" Do you want some more tea now ? Let
me pour it, please."

" You can pour the cream in, the teapot is
too hot and too heavy."

"I saw a pillow-case in the garden this morning," continued Babs, when the new tea was ready.

"A what ? "

"A pillow-case ; you know, what crawls."

"I don't understand you ; what was it like ? " Her uncle could not imagine what she meant.

"It was brown, and furry, and creepy, like a velvet worm."

"You mean a caterpillar."

"Oh, yes ! that's it. I knew there was a pilla' in it somewhere. On wet days I see black snails too. Mrs. Forrester wants 'Lizabeth Lamb to swallow black snails for her decline, but she won't never."

"She's right there," laughed the captain.

"Now you've finished your breakfus' shall we go out ? " asked Babs, confidingly slipping her hand into her uncle's. "I can show you the garden, you know."

"All right ; only bring me a match first."

But Captain Conway could not get over his little niece's personal appearance. He had always felt so sure that Barbara's daughter would be a beauty, and both he and his pretty, empty-headed wife had been influenced in their idea of taking the children to live with them

for a while by such poor thin thoughts as these
—a lovely, well-dressed little girl, seated beside
her aunt in the victoria, a sweet, gentle play-
thing for dull afternoons, a striking little couple
to introduce into children's parties.   The boy
was the heir so his appearance did not matter
much, still it was a great pleasure to find him
so handsome and taking—but the girl!   Silly
Aunt Eleanor was quite looking forward to
showing off her pretty little niece, to taking her
out with her, and dressing her exquisitely.
And Captain Conway was thinking of all this,
when he looked at Babs.   He was young and
silly also.   Accustomed to talk by the hour
about a woman's points, and the fit of her
frock, and how she looked, and walked, and
rode, and danced.   And he, too, had never
imagined such a catastrophe as a plain relation.
His mother had been a beauty, his wife was one
of course.   His sister-in-law was really lovely,
and his niece—she who was to take the place
which a little daughter of his own would have
filled, was quite the plainest, most common-
looking child he had ever noticed ; at least so
he decided in his impatient disappointment.
Her shrill, quaint talk was certainly amusing
now in the Cloverdale garden, but her uncle

shuddered at the thought of "Giles," or
"'Lizabeth Lamb and her decline," being mentioned with that accent in the Onslow Square
drawing-room.   A governess must be immediately procured.

"Can you read?" he asked suddenly, a
question suggested by the idea of the governess.

Babs was lying flat on her face in the grass,
trying to see down a mole-hole.

"On'y a bit," she answered, adding gaily :
"Teddy can, kite well, an' he makes poentry,
too, splendid poentry!   Shall I tell you his
best piece?"

"By all means," said the captain, lighting
another cigarette.

Babs folded her grimy fingers, and repeated
the following remarkable verse :—

> "'Let's learn Latin, Vochasafe,
> Learn it quickly as you can ;
> And he dashed the sparkling water
> At the feet of Mary Ann'.

Isn't that a splendid one?"

The captain laughed.

"What do you mean by Vochasafe?" he
asked.

"He's Teddy's favourite man in church,

don't you know, what we sing about? He comes near the end of a rather long singin', and Teddy and I always listen out for him, but he's Teddy's favourite. Mine in church is ' Harry Lujah,' but he on'y comes sometimes."

" Do you like going to church ? "

" Oh, yes ! all 'cept the beseeches. But I made a piece of poentry, too, on'y it's not such a nice one. It's :—

> ' There was a little girl,
> And she had a yellow frock,
> And she had a pella lock '."

" That's a very nice one," said Uncle Charley, " only I don't quite know what a ' pella lock ' is ? "

Babs looked rather doubtful.

" A lock is what's in the doors, you see, and my little Marys cover them."

" Your little what ? "

" My little Marys, I call them, they're rather like wooden people, and the key pushes them aside. I kiss them often."

" This is a most remarkable specimen," thought the captain, as Babs rushed off in pursuit of a butterfly ; " I never heard such a rigmarole in my life. They must be most extraordinary children."

But there Captain Conway showed his ig-
norance of children.　Teddy and Babs only
thought, and talked, and lived as thousands of
other imaginative children do, in the happy
interesting world of pretence.　Uncle Charley
had made the mistake in thinking that the
children would be big dolls, so of course he
was astonished to find that they were really
little men and women.

"Babs," he called, sitting down on a garden
seat, "would you like me to take you to Teddy
in London, and to see Aunt Eleanor?"

"The sooner she's in a civilised atmosphere
the better," he thought to himself.

But apparently Babs did not hear him.　She
was dancing excitedly round and round a small
object on the path, and screaming: "My catter!
my catter!" with great delight.

Uncle Charley perceived that she had again
met with her friend the caterpillar.

"Babs," he repeated, "would you like me to
take you to London?"

"Oh, yes!" cried the child, diverted directly.
"I want to go to London awful much.　Giles
has told me all 'bout it."

"Well, we'll go to-morrow.　One of the
housemaids can take you."

" But you said you'd take me."

" So I will, but you'd go in another carriage, you see."

" How funny," laughed Babs. " Will there be more'n one carriage ? It'll be a nice surprise for Nana and Teddy when I come. I like you, Uncle Charley, much better'n I did at first," she continued earnestly, " though you see, you are rather a 'pointment to me, when I 'spected a fat soldier with a trumpet. But Giles says use is second nature, and I guess we've got used to each other. Was I a 'pointment to you, Uncle Charley ? "

" Suppose I expected a fair little girl with golden hair and blue eyes ! " said the captain, reverting to his late vision.

" Oh ! Uncle Charley, did you really ? " she cried ; and there was a pathos in her tone that drowned the provincial accent, and caused her uncle to kiss her hurriedly, and suggest a visit to Giles to tell him of her journey to London, which happily diverted Babs for the moment. But alas ! the created thought lived on in the child's soul.

The next morning all was bustle and confusion—quite a new experience to Babs. The servants kept kissing her whenever they met

her, instead of telling her not to bother, and
after she had gone old Giles's tears fell fast on
the geranium plant which he was trying to pot.

Babs could not understand why every one at
Cloverdale made such a sudden fuss about her.
She was only going to London, just to find
Teddy and her Aunt Eleanor. She had no
idea that the dear old home was to be shut up,
and nearly all the servants sent away, until that
far-away, unreal father and mother of hers came
back from India, and nobody quite knew when
that would be.

" Take care of the eggs, be sure ! " she said
the last thing, as the servants stood waving
their hands, and the final piece of luggage was
being put on to the carriage ; " and if the little
birds come while I'm away, be very kind to
them, and don't punish them, even if they do
wrong. Good-bye, dear Giles ! good-bye."

" Thank heaven, that is over without a storm
of tears," thought Uncle Charley, with a sigh
of relief, as he watched Babs pointing out to a
wretched little Dutch doll all the beauties of
the scenery on the road, with the brightest
possible face. " What a mercy, she doesn't
mind about going. I was afraid she would
have fretted awfully."

It did not strike Uncle Charley that she did not understand that she was really leaving her old home for a time ; and that, as a child, she was incapable of looking beyond the near horizon of the hour.

The immediate interests of first the drive to the station, and then the long railway journey, entirely filled her mind.   The excitement of sandwiches in the train, and then of waking after a long sleep, still to find herself rushing along through the country, drove all thoughts of the home left behind out of her head.   She could not remember much about the journey after to tell Teddy—it left a confusion of impressions which she could not disentangle. She was rather sleepy too, when they at last left the train, and she took little notice of the drive through the streets to Onslow Square.

Nana and Teddy were in the hall of the strange house, and the old nurse snatched up her darling and carried her straight off upstairs, such a long, long way up to a funny small nursery, where nice bread and milk was ready, and a cosy cot beside Nana's bed.

Aunt Eleanor was out just then, and it was too high up for her to go to the nursery afterwards to see her new little niece.

"You had better know the worst at once,
Nora," said her husband, as they sat down to
dinner that night. "She is an awfully plain,
rough, wild little creature, not half as nicely
behaved as the boy. I can't believe she's
Barbara's child."

"Oh, what a pity! I don't like any children
much, and I detest rough, naughty ones! We
must get a governess at once. That silly old
nurse spoils them frightfully, I can see."

"She's a clever little thing, though! She
kept me amused the whole of yesterday."

"Clever! worse and worse, Charley! I do
hate a clever, plain girl more than I can tell
you! Oh, I do wish she had been a doll!
I've told such a lot of people about the little
niece that I'm going to have, and now I
shall be ashamed to show her, from what you
say."

"Yes you will, I'm afraid. But she can live
in the nursery."

"Good gracious, yes! I shan't bother with
her. If she'd been like Barbara now, I would
have taken her about with me, and it would
have been fun to have dressed her. I like the
look of a pretty little girl in a victoria. People
would have thought she was my own who saw

us driving. Do I look old enough, Charley, to have a daughter of five?"

"Rather not! But really I am sorry about the child, though it can't be helped. It is still more vexing for Ned and Barbara than for us! We'd better have the child photographed and send it out to them, to break it to them gently."

And poor little Babs was dreaming of the big, bright home behind her, utterly unconscious of the new, narrow life which she was to live in the sunless atmosphere of her uncle and aunt's selfish life.

# CHAPTER III.

## IN LONDON.

" LONDON isn't nearly as big as the country," said Babs one day, pressing her nose flat against the window.

" How do you know?" asked Teddy.

" By looking, of course. At home we could see the garden, then the field, and the woods and the hills ever so far away, what was generally bluish. And here you just see nothing but the streets, and there's no far-away at all."

" I like London," said Teddy, " 'cause you see soldiers sometimes, and it's fun driving in the park."

" I've never drived in the park yet," announced Babs rather mournfully. "And I don't like always going walks and wearing gloves."

" Gloves are horrid!" agreed her brother.

"And Aunt Eleanor says I must always wear them!" very sadly. "And it's so hot, my fingers is all sticky and tight in them."

KENSINGTON GARDENS.

"There seems more children in London than the country," Teddy thought.

"But we don't never play with them. I asked Aunt Eleanor if I mightn't play with some of them in Kensington Gardens, and she said certainly not or I'd catch something."

"What?" asked Teddy.

"She didn't say. But it seems a pity not to play when there are such lots of children!"

"Now, Miss Babs dear," called Nana, "come and have your things on and we'll go for a walk. Wace is coming too." Wace was Aunt Eleanor's maid. Babs was a very different-looking child now to what she used to be at Cloverdale. No comfortable dirty pinafore was allowed in London, but a clean white frock with a wide black sash. Thin shiny shoes and silk stockings instead of the old thick boots and cotton socks; and a big hat trimmed very smartly on the top of her well-brushed hair. But Aunt Eleanor still thought her woefully plain, and took far more notice of pretty Teddy, who looked charming in his new sailor suits.

"Let's go up to the park!" said Teddy as they started out.

"Oh, yes!" cried Babs enthusiastically; "'cause we might see the soldiers."

Soldiers are one of the few things in London
that really attract the attention of children.    In
the country they notice almost everything they
see ;  but  in  London  probably  the  mass  of
objects  prevent  most  of  them  from  being
individualised,  and  children  walk  along  apparently  unconscious  of  the  vast  stream  of
traffic, the army of horses, the endless number
of people, the thousand objects in fact that line
one's  way  through  London.   Every  now  and
then they notice a really interesting thing, such
as a watering cart, or a barrel organ, especially
if crowned  by  a  monkey, or, above  all  things,
the  ordinary  London  cat.    That  is  always
exciting—whether asleep  on  the  area  steps, or
peeping through  the  railings, or  taking  a  con-
stitutional walk, or chatting  with  a  neighbour.
A child will never  pass by a cat without seeing
it, feeling a personal interest in it, and probably
hanging  behind  on  the  nurse's  hand  to  get  a
last look at so dear a feline friend.

Teddy  and  Babs  were  no  exception  to  the
rule.    They walked up Queen's Gate and saw
hardly  anything  therein.    A  man  mending  a
lamp-post at last attracted Teddy's attention,
and  he  and  Babs  suddenly  developed  an
interest in lamp-posts.

"Do you fink he's the man what turns out the London gas in the morning?" said Babs. "Oh, I would like to ask him!"

"Come along, Miss Babs dear," called nurse.

Just then they saw a really very entertaining thing. A sparrow flying along with a huge straw in its mouth, which instantly produced in Babs a perfect frenzy of delight.

"Oh look, look!" she cried. "Nana, Wace, do look at that dear little bird what has got the straw! I 'spects he's going to build a nest like the birds do in the country. Where do you fink he lives?"

"Somewhere quite near, Miss Babs," said Wace. "Very likely in that tree."

"Do you fink he's the one I hear chirping in the mornings?" asked the child.

"Bless her little heart!" ejaculated nurse. Poor Nana found London rather tiring after the peaceful rest of Cloverdale, and moreover she was always longing for the big garden for the children to play in.

"Squares indeed!" she had scornfully observed, "they be but poor shoddy imitations of real gardens!"

Teddy and Babs were talking eagerly about

the sparrow when Wace called their attention excitedly :—

" Look, Miss Babs and Master Teddy, there is the Princess of Wales ! "

Teddy looked hurriedly at a passing omnibus and Babs straight up in the air, as if she were hoping to see the princess in a balloon. By the time their attention was properly directed they succeeded in catching sight of the back of a far-distant carriage, and were not suitably impressed.

Then they crossed over into the park, and Teddy and Babs began to run. Teddy was a soldier on a horse—one of those dear ones that the Life Guards ride—his black trousers carried out that idea, and his hat on one side made a splendid soldier ; and Babs was a train. It must have been warm work rushing about in the sun on a broiling June day in addition to keeping up a perpetual puffing and blowing, but that was of course necessary to the idea of the train.

By-and-by the sound of distant music and gleam of far-off colour intimated that the soldiers were really coming up Queen's Gate on their way back to the Knightsbridge Barracks.

Shrieks of delight from Babs attracted the amused attention of several passers-by.

" How lovely they was ! " she said when the show was over. " I likes the soldiers better than anything in London."

" Of course I do ! " agreed Teddy.

" Uncle Charley is not so much of a soldier as we 'fought, is he, Teddy ? I've never seen him like one yet."

" You forget his medal, Babs."

" I s'pose so—but when a man's never a thing you forget what he really is," said the little girl lucidly.

" He is going to a reg'mental dinner to-night, and he will wear his soldier things."

" I likes soldiers what fights better than those that on'y go out to dinner."

" I like both kinds," said Teddy, who had a well-regulated masculine mind.

" Let's find things," suggested Babs, and that was a game which never fell flat. Such wonderful treasures they found in Kensington Gardens ! A broken bit of shell on the pathway, the outside of a horse-chestnut under the trees, a piece of fancy grass that was growing, and a hundred other things which none but children's eyes would have noticed, and which would have brought pleasure to none but children's souls.

The morning was gone in no time, and Babs and Teddy were surprised when Nana said that it was time to go home to dinner. And there a new treat awaited them. A lady had written to ask Aunt Eleanor to bring the children to a garden party she was giving that afternoon.

"Will you be good if I take you?" her aunt asked Babs. There was generally a gritty sound in Aunt Eleanor's voice when she spoke to her little niece. She was always irritated with the child for not being pretty, and she never tried to understand Babs's eager, original nature. She did not mean to be actually unkind, only she was utterly ignorant of how great a depth of sympathy and knowledge is needed by those who have the care of little children.

"Oh, I will be good, I promise!" said Babs excitedly. "I won't do nothing at all naughty."

"Very well! Now go and tell nurse to dress you in your very best!"

At four o'clock they started in the carriage, to the children's keen delight. Babs chattered unceasingly.

"Do you fink they remembers to feed all the omdibus horses?" she asked. "Oh, look, Teddy! at that old man getting up that omdibus—he 'minds me so much of Giles!"

" Don't point, Babs," said her aunt sharply.
" That is not behaving at all well."

" I'm so sorry, I didn't know ! " said Babs,
with a cloud over her bright face, " but how do
you make people see fings if you don't point ? "

Aunt Eleanor could not bear the trouble of
answering children's questions.

" Do be quiet a bit," she said testily.

And a ten seconds' silence ensued.

" Wace's young man used to conduck in an
omdibus," began the little girl again, " but he
left to better himself."

" What an awful child she is," thought Aunt
Eleanor ; " I wish I had only brought Teddy ! "

But Babs was quite unconscious of her
crimes.

Happily the drive soon came to an end, and
directly they were safely inside the garden Aunt
Eleanor forgot all about the children and went
off with several friends whom she had not seen
during the whole dreary month in which she
had been obliged to mourn for her husband's
mother. Teddy too behaved rather shabbily
to Babs. The hostess brought two little boys
to play with him, and after staring at each
other for a while, after the manner of children,
the bigger of the two observed :—

4

" Come on ! "

And Teddy went—leaving his sister alone on
the terrace.   But Babs was a dear, sunny, little
soul, who was wont to make the best of everything, and though her childish spirits sank at
the sad experience of not being a big boy like
Teddy, she soon cheered up and began to talk
to a nice lady with a kind face who had seen
the baby tragedy, and was full of sympathy for
the little girl.

" Would you like some strawberries, dear ? "
she asked—and Babs's face brightened wonderfully as she slipped her hand into that of her
new friend.

" I'se never been to a real grown-up party
afore," she said confidingly, " 'cause we lived
in the country always."

" I expect you like the country better than
London," said the lady.

" I likes them both—but the country is my
fav'rite.   You see in London I have to wear
gloves, and it matters 'bout not being pretty.
I never knowed in the country that I wasn't."

The lady looked quite sad all in a minute
and Babs thought there were tears in her eyes.

" Where's your mother, dear ? " she asked
gently.

"In Inja. She's coming home soon. I've never see'd my mother nor father, and Teddy has forgotten them, but Nana remembers them."

"I'm so glad she is coming!" said the lady. "I used to live in the country too, but that was a long time ago."

"When you was in your last place?" suggested Babs.

The lady laughed.

"Yes, darling," she said. "And now tell me if your little brother is kind to you?"

"Oh yes! We always play together, unless," and her face clouded over again, "unless there's any bigger children what makes me too little."

"You'll be bigger some day, you know."

"It'll never be no good," continued Babs mournfully, "'cause when I'se seven he'll be nine."

"Never mind that. Have some more strawberries, or a piece of cake."

"I aren't messing at all, are I?" asked the little girl anxiously, "'cause I promised Aunt Eleanor I'd be good."

"You are very good, dear," said the lady.

"Yesterday was a bad day for Uncle Charley," began Babs when the cake was finished and she had gone with her new friend for a walk

round the garden, "his best shirts was messed
in the wash. Teddy and I was playing after
tea, and we was so happy in the passage, when
all of a sudden Uncle Charley came out of his
dressing-room with a crumpled shirt and he was
so angry!—as angry as—as—a lion what has
missed a person."

"Here is a swing," said the lady, smiling at
these domestic revelations, "would you like to
get on it?"

"Oh yes!" screamed Babs, to whom the
swing was a dear country sight.

"I'll swing you," said the lady.

"Oh no! Don't touch me! I can do it all
right. We had a swing at Cloverdale. Look!"
as the swing began to move in obedience
to her extreme efforts, "I are quite a little
acrowboat."

The lady laughed again.

"You are indeed!" she said. "But you will
get so hot, let me swing you now!" So Babs
had a lovely swing.

"I are 'joying myself," she said in a glad
little voice.

"Is your country home very far away?"
asked her friend.

"Oh yes, thousand of miles! There was a

stone in the road what said 'one hundred and ninety-five miles to London'. Would that mean this London, do you fink?"

"Yes, dear."

"Well, it was all that far away. We'll go home again some day when Father-and-Mother-in-Inja come, if there's a train to take us."

"There will certainly be a train," the lady assured her.

Just then a young man joined them.

"How are you, Mrs. Alison? I didn't know you were here; and what a very nice person you have got to talk to!"

"She is quite splendid!" Then to Babs— "This gentleman likes little girls".

"On'y pretty ones?" asked Babs pathetically.

"Only fat, happy, funny ones," said the young man, "just like you."

"That's a good fing!" laughed Babs. "I are kite fat, an' shall I show you what makes me happy?"

"Yes, do! What is it?"

Babs turned out her tiny pocket. It contained a clean pocket-handkerchief, and a small paper parcel. She opened the paper and proudly displayed what was apparently a bit of meat.

"It's the tip of a tongue," she explained.
"Teddy and I got one for luck, you know.
Cook gived it us, and sometimes I carry it and
sometimes he does. It brought us the soldiers
this morning, and a party this afternoon. One
tip lasts 'bout a fortnight; but if you wear
cotton frocks you have to be very careful to
remember to take it out of your pocket afore
it's sent to the wash."

"That's a good superstition!" said the young
man to the lady, and then they both laughed.

"You're a rum little creature!" he said to
Babs.

"Will any one be wanting you, dear?" asked
the lady. "I think we had better go back to
the terrace."

"Oh, yes, p'r'aps Aunt Eleanor and Teddy.
Is the party over?" in a doleful tone.

"Well it is nearly. I am going home now."

"And I am," added the young man.

"Good gracious, child, where have you
been?" exclaimed Aunt Eleanor impatiently,
and then seeing Mrs. Alison—"I hope my little
niece hasn't been boring you".

"Oh, no," said the lady, "I like her." And
as Aunt Eleanor hurried away with the children, Mrs, Alison said to the young man;

"Aunt Eleanor would have bored me to death in five minutes, but that nice little niece of hers —never!"

"Good-bye, kind lady," said Babs, running back and holding up her face for a kiss, "I hope I'll see you every day."

"Good-bye!" called the young man. "What is your name? you never told me."

"Curdie!" shouted Babs as her aunt called her. For Mrs. Conway's carriage stopped the way.

"A most 'strordinary thing happened to me," began the little girl as they drove off, "a gentleman spoke to me what I did not know. He asked me my name, but I thought I had better not tell him, so I said Curdie."

"How silly you are!" said Aunt Eleanor.

"Were those two nice little boys?" to Teddy.

"Middlin'!" answered Teddy. "They're going to school soon. When am I going to school, Auntie?"

"When you know a little more. A governess is coming for you and Babs on Monday— and then we shall see how you get on."

"Shall I go to Eton school, like those other boys?"

" I expect so. But your father will decide
when he comes home."

" What'll I do when Teddy goes to school ? "
asked Babs with a dawning fear.

But nobody took the trouble to answer her.
Teddy was thinking of the new world of school,
and Aunt Eleanor was nodding to a friend.

When they reached home it was almost the
children's bed-time, but they were so anxious to
see Uncle Charley dressed in his soldier things
that they were allowed to stay downstairs.

Aunt Eleanor put on a tea-gown, and threw
herself down on the sofa.

" I feel . wretchedly ill ! " she exclaimed
petulantly, " these hot days give me such a
headache ! "

" Do you fink you'll get better or die ? "
asked Babs with interest.

" She is the most unfeeling child I ever
saw ! " thought her aunt—but aloud she said
snappishly :—

" Of course I shall get better ! "

" I'm so glad ! "

Just then a telegram was brought in asking
Mrs. Conway to dine with some people in a
friendly way and go with them to their box at
the opera afterwards,

The headache vanished as if by magic. She, poor, pleasure-loving soul, was only sick of stopping at home; and she rushed upstairs to dress in the greatest delight. Uncle Charley came down first, and the children danced round him in a perfect ecstasy.

"How lovely you look!" cried Babs, "a regular pride o' the nation!"

"And your medal on too!" said Teddy; "why don't you wear it always?"

"A hansom!" said their uncle to the butler, while Babs was stroking his sleeve and kissing his sword.

"Good-night, little people!" patting their heads. Uncle Charley always treated the children as if they were dogs—not prize ones of course—but nice common-place dogs, who occasionally were brought out of their kennels for a treat.

"I likes Uncle Charley better than Aunt Eleanor," said Babs as the hansom drove away.

"And I do," agreed Teddy, "'cause he's a soldier."

"An' kinder," added the little girl.

"Oh!" This last remark had reference to their aunt, whom they now saw in evening dress for the first time. She had not been to a party

since they came, besides they were always in
bed before her dinner-time.

She really did look beautiful. The jetted
black dress showed off the fairness of her com-
plexion, and diamonds flashed in her golden
hair.

"You're as lovely as a fairy," said Teddy
admiringly, "or an angel!"

Aunt Eleanor kissed him and looked pleased.

"How splendid you do look!" exclaimed
Babs after a deep-drawn breath. "Giles always
said Uncle Charley had married one as would
be more for ornament than use—and you are,
aren't you?"

Her aunt's pretty face quite changed.

"How often am I to forbid you to repeat that
odious old Giles's chatter?" she said angrily.
For the exact reproduction of the old gardener's
accent was most offensive to her fastidious ears,
and besides the vulgar truth of his saying was
hardly palatable.

The child's bright happy look faded. It was
rather a sad little Babs that waved her good-
night from the window.

Sad thoughts had begun to come to the little
girl in this new life of hers. She knew she
continually vexed her aunt, and yet at the time

she was unconscious of any wrong. She read the impatience of Aunt Eleanor's tone and the disapprobation of her glance in the midst of the merriest play ; and exceeding bitter once was her cry : " All the little girls are pretty 'cept me ! " after she had seen her aunt lavishing admiration and petting on Lady Eveleigh's golden-haired, doll-faced children. And yet she bore no grudge against Aunt Eleanor, nor yet against Teddy, whom both uncle and aunt so obviously preferred. Few people who saw this common-place, sturdy little maiden would have guessed the depth and beauty of her fair child-soul.

# CHAPTER IV.

### NURSERY LIFE.

It was very different playing in the London nursery, far away up so many stairs, and shut in even from the interests of the landing by a little wooden gate that Teddy could not open, much less Babs, to having the big old house and glorious garden at Cloverdale all to themselves.

There were no delightful corners in this stiff, straight room wherein the children could crouch, and bump their heads, and enjoy themselves in a hundred enchanting, imaginary ways. No beautiful cupboards in which to hide, nor sofa-arms to ride upon, as there were in the dear old nursery at home.

But the children accepted the existing as the inevitable, in which they were wiser than some of their elders, and made the best of their new cramped quarters.

" If there isn't room enough for hare-and-hounds there is for giving a party," said Babs

NURSERY DAYS.

brightly. "Will you give one, or shall I, Teddy?"

"I will," answered Teddy, "only we must ask Nana for things to eat."

"You might live in the night nursery," suggested Babs, "and then I could come to the party kite proper."

"And you wouldn't know what there was to eat till you arrived," said Teddy, "that's like a real party."

"It's a bit dull for me while you is getting it ready," complained Babs. "Couldn't I pretend I was your cook, just till it was ready for the party to arrive?"

"Would you forget you knew, and be very surprised?" asked Teddy doubtfully.

"Oh, I would, I promise!" pleaded Babs; so she was allowed to assist in the preparation of the great feast. The pity of it was that they could not go down into the kitchen here as they would have done at Cloverdale, to coax really splendid eatables, such as a handful of currants and a piece of candied peel, out of the good-natured old cook. They had to be content with what Nana could give them, but it was a lovely feast all the same, in spite of rather a scarceness of provisions.

It was laid out in a little dinner set belonging
to Babs, instead of the usual tea set, because,
as Teddy said : " The things we've got to eat
are more dinnery than teaish ".

Two glass decanters were filled with water
tinged pink by the introduction of a little tooth-
powder, of which mixture Babs was very proud.

" It makes a splendid wine," she screamed,
clapping her hands.  Two cough lozenges made
a show at one end of the table, and a piece of
liquorice cut up with the scissors out of Nana's
work-basket at the other.  A dish of brown
sugar well moistened with warm water made an
attractive sweet, but the crowning glory of the
feast was a pile of camphor pills borrowed from
Nana on the understanding that neither of the
children would eat them.  Babs could not
resist just touching one with her tongue, but
it very quickly dried again, and Nana never
knew.

" Good-morning, Captain Teddy," said the
little visitor pleasantly, on her admission.  She
looked quite gorgeous in a night-cap of Nana's,
and an antimacassar over her shoulders.

" Good-morning, Mrs. Babs," solemnly replied Teddy, who had a black corked moustache and whiskers.

"How do you do, and how are your children?" continued the lady vivaciously.

"Quite well, thank you, ma'am, and how are yours?"

Teddy was never so good at originating conversation as Babs.

"One of them is dead," answered the visitor cheerfully, "her head came off this morning when I dropped her. I have brought my best daughter with me, you see," and she displayed with pride her last new doll.

"Take a seat," said Teddy in a gruff voice.

Babs sat down at the table,—which was not a table at all, but the lower half of her high chair which unscrewed in the middle ;—and the feast began.

"The cough lozenges taste of having a cold. I don't like them," said Babs, forgetting her party manners.

"It is very rude to say so!" observed Teddy, looking rather cross.

"Oh, I beg your pardon!" exclaimed Babs, who never wished to vex her brother. She would have said "I'se sorry," if she had not been Mrs. Babs out at a party. Teddy was carving the liquorice and did not reply.

"You ought to say 'granted' like Mrs.

5

Forrester used," said the little girl.  "It's manners!"

"The visitor oughtn't to tell the gentleman that's giving the party what to say," argued Teddy.

Babs hastily changed the subject.

"Dear Captain Teddy," she said in a funny grave voice, "might I trouble you for another help of that 'licious sugar slop?"

Peace was instantly restored, and the feast finished without another hitch.

"The tooth-powder wine is a little bitter," Teddy observed on his own account, but he drained the last drop manfully.

The London nursery did quite nicely too for playing rabbits in.

"We was always wild rabbits at Cloverdale, but we can be tame ones here like our own ones in the pen at home," suggested Babs; and so pretending to be rabbits would not have been spoiled at all, if Nana had not mentioned the fact that Babs's black silk stockings would wear out at the knees, and then Aunt Eleanor was very cross and forbade any more creeping on hands and knees.  That was a dire disappointment to Babs, because creeping was so much nicer and more interesting than just dull walking properly.

To make up, kind Nana sometimes let them play rabbits at night in bed, where they could creep and burrow, and it was altogether delightful !

But the chief game which the children played in London was that of the toy people. They could not continue the Stoner romance at all well in such a small room, and besides the Stoners had stayed at Cloverdale. So they turned their pretending life into that of the toy people, who lived for the most part in brick houses built on the ottoman, and had themselves all originally sprung from sundry Noah's arks.

There were four great families of them—the Reds, the Yellows, the Browns, and the Blues, and each family consisted of a big Mr. and Mrs. who were the grand-parents ; a little Mr. and Mrs. who were the parents, and such children as the remainder of the Noah's arks supplied. Of course the families were not all intact. For instance, big Mrs. Yellow had found an early grave down a grating in the Cloverdale garden, from which there was no possibility of rescue, and little Mrs. Brown had met with a violent death in the jaws of Don the retriever. A very awkward thing too had

happened to one of the young Yellows.   Babs
dropped him by mistake into the bath, and
when the water was wiped off him, the yellow
came off too, so he became an outcast from
his family, and took a situation as White, the
footman, in a distinguished family called Violet,
which belonged to Teddy.   Not of Noah's ark
origin were these, but out of a most aristocratic
toy-box.   The Violets had figures and features
of their own, and were consequently called lord
and lady by the admiring children.   It was
rather a sore point with Babs that Teddy insisted on " doing for " the Violets entirely.   It
seemed so cheerless to the little girl to be thus
shut out of their stately home.

Occasionally the original families were broken
up, and a coalition household formed, but the
most popular game was in the varied fortunes
of the four families themselves.

Babs's favourite person was a dear grown-up
daughter of the Yellows', aged sixteen—and
the child loved that thin bit of painted wood,
called Annie Yellow, with a love that her
mother was hungry for away in India.

On week days the toy children all attended a
school kept by big Mr. Brown, and on Sundays
Teddy built a beautiful church, and Babs had

splendid fun making Dicky Blue behave badly,
or laying little Mrs. Red low with a sudden
and dangerous complaint called the " rheumatic
'sterics ".

One day a terrible thing happened. When
the children were putting away the toy people,
Jane Red was missing. High and low they
searched, but in vain.

" I can't sleep for finking of poor Jane," said
Babs, after she had been in bed about three
minutes.

" Never mind, dearie," said Nana soothingly ;
" we'll find her to-morrow all right."

So Babs's sleepless night of anxiety came to
an end before Nana went to her supper, though
the little girl's first thought in the morning was
for the missing toy maiden.

And, sad to relate, the nursery maid in
sweeping had found the unhappy Jane under
the ottoman with her head severed from her
body.

" She's kite dead," said Babs sadly.

" We must have a funeral then," suggested
Teddy, and this exciting idea instantly raised
Babs's spirits.

The coal-box was selected as a suitable tomb,
and thither the defunct Jane was solemnly

borne, wrapped up in a bit of newspaper. As
an appropriate dirge, Teddy sang, " Rosalie
the Prairie Flower " ; Babs joining in where
she knew the words.

When the excitement of the obsequies had
abated, Teddy still further rejoiced Babs's soul,
by intimating that the Red family must go into
mourning, and, after a little coaxing, nurse lent
them a pen and ink, with which they proceeded
to make a black girdle round all the principal
Reds and their collaterals.

" I'm glad Jane was killed," announced
heartless Teddy, the pen and ink proved so
enthralling.

"Oh, Teddy !" exclaimed Babs reproachfully ; " how can you ? But still, now she is
dead, all this busyness keeps us from frettin'.
But I'm 'fraid Alice Blue will miss her very
bad."

" They always were friends, I know," said
Teddy solemnly.

" P'r'aps Alice might have mourning too,"
suggested Babs brightly, when the Reds were
all dry.

That was a very happy thought, and Teddy
delighted his little sister's soul by allowing her
to do Alice all by herself, which resulted in a

few blots and stains on frock and hands, but
an amount of bliss which far outweighed such
trifles.

"I fink it 'ud be nice for the Reds to
have another child to make up for poor
Jane," observed Babs, regarding the stricken
family on the table, "and I've got a fought,
Teddy."

"What is it?" asked her brother.

"You know White, the Violets' footman?
Mightn't we dip him in the red ink what's in
the library, and make him a new son for little
Mr. and Mrs. Red?"

"Do you think Uncle Charley would let
us?"

"Aunt Eleanor wouldn't, but Uncle Charley
might if we asked him as a great treat."

"Anyhow we can try," said Teddy; and
hand in hand the solemn little couple trotted
down the long staircase and gently knocked at
the library door.

Uncle Charley was yawning just then. He
had finished smoking, at least as much as he
ever finished; and his letters were written; and
there were no books to read—that is, no yellow-
backs, which were Uncle Charley's idea of
books; and it was raining; and there was a

whole hour to get through before he went down
to the club.   He was just wondering whatever
he could do to amuse himself when the children's
rap attracted his attention.

It was a most propitious moment for Teddy
and Babs.

"What do you want, youngsters?" Uncle
Charley asked smiling.

"Oh, please," they began in one breath,
and then Babs finished, "might we dip the
footman in your red ink?"

Uncle Charley looked amused.   "What do
you mean?" he asked.

"It's like this," continued Babs earnestly,
and their funny sober faces made Uncle Charley
laugh.   "The Reds have lost their daughter
Jane what died under the ottoman in the night,
and we fink a new grown-up son would cheer
them up, poor fings!"

"Yes, poor things!" chimed in Teddy; "I'll
tell the rest, Babs.   So we want you please to
let us dip White, the Violets' footman, in your
red ink—do let us!"

"Yes, do, dear uncle!" pleaded Babs, "and
then he'll make a very nice young Red."

"All right," said Uncle Charley, "only perhaps I'd better dip him."

" Oh yes ! " screamed the children, " how kind you are ! "

" I like you very much ! " exclaimed Babs, dancing about in her excitement. So the little white wooden man was made a bright red, and Uncle Charley delighted the children still further by inking him a nose, mouth, and eyes.

" Shall I give him a moustache ? " he asked.

" I don't fink sons ever have moustaches," said Babs doubtfully, " only uncles and fathers."

" He's quite the handsomest of all the toy people now," observed Teddy, looking admiringly at his uncle's handiwork.

" He's the only one with a mouth," piped in Babs. " Oh, fank you so much, dear uncle ! "

" Yes, thanks awfully ! " said Teddy.

And then as Uncle Charley had nothing else to do, he played with the children for a little, and made them a paper boat out of a sheet of writing-paper, and a tiny cocked hat.

" You'se awful clever," said his little niece admiringly ; " I don't fink there's another man in London what is so clever and so kind."

Uncle Charley was quite pleased with their devotion.

" I'm glad we make the children so happy,"

he thought to himself. " I must tell Ned about them when I write. It will please him and Barbara."

The next time there was a catastrophe among the toy people, and Barry Brown's hat was licked white by the dog, of course the children knew where to go to have it set right.

"Uncle Charley will do it for us," said Teddy confidently.

"Oh, yes!" agreed Babs; "he will be sure to do it. I'm glad we've got an uncle what is so kind. It makes there always a help for fings."

"We will go now and get it done," said Teddy, and he and his little sister tore downstairs, and hardly waited for an answer to their rap before they rushed into the library.

"We've brought Barry——" began Babs, but then she saw that Uncle Charley, who was leaning back in a chair, was scowling dreadfully.

"Now then, you youngsters! Clear out of here, and look sharp about it!" he said angrily.

"What's the matter?" gasped the little girl.

"Do you hear what I say? How dare you stand staring there when I have told you to go? Be off at once, and don't come bothering down here again!"

The children rushed upstairs in a panic. They could not know that some very persistent tradesmen had insisted on immediate payment of their bills, and Uncle Charley had ordered them out of the house in a fury, being ready to vent his superfluous anger on the first objects that turned up, which unfortunately were poor little Babs and Teddy.

" What was we naughty about? " asked Babs breathlessly.

" I expect it was going downstairs without being sent for," Teddy thought.

" But we went the other day, and Uncle Charley wasn't a bit angry."

" That does make it puzzling," answered Teddy doubtfully.

" If it had been Aunt Eleanor I shouldn't have been 'prised," said Babs sadly, " but Uncle Charley what used to be so kind ! "

" He isn't kind now," observed Teddy.

" Don't you fink he ever will be again ? "

" He may. Grown-ups often change, you know."

" I hopes Uncle Charley will, but I should be too frightened to go down again to see."

" And I should."

" Do you fink Father-and-Mother-in-Inja will

be at all like Uncle Charley and Aunt Eleanor ? " asked Babs a little anxiously.

" I expect so," said Teddy gloomily.

" I don't fink I likes fathers and mothers and
uncles and aunts," whimpered Babs. " It was
much nicer in the country with just Giles and
all the lambs and chickens and fings. I'se tired
of London ! "

Poor little people ! It was so easy to make
the sun shine in the nursery, and cross, selfish
Uncle Charley had hidden it all away with his
ugly thundercloud, and then he went down to
the club and forgot all about it.

# CHAPTER V.

## ABOUT LESSONS.

THE new governess had come, and lessons were quite a fresh experience for Teddy and Babs. Nana used to teach Teddy to read and write, and Babs had learned a little of both too, but on the whole they were very ignorant children for seven and five years old.

Miss Grimston was a real old-fashioned governess—very prim, and proper, and particular. Thoroughly imbued with that most absurd of dying theories, that children should be seen and not heard—just as if their fresh original chatter were not one of the most delightful things to be found in life, and the expression of their quaint baby thoughts one of the most entertaining. Moreover she laboured under the delusion that it is better to drag out and punish all the current naughtiness of the nursery, than just simply and quietly to look the other way ; to extract continuous confessions of unreal sorrow for unrepented-of

deeds, instead of diverting the child's thoughts
and feelings into another better channel, and
letting well alone when you have done so.

Miss Grimston was an excellent person;
conscientious down to the heels of her flat little
boots, and invaluable in carrying out any work
which she undertook—provided it was not the
education of children, for which she was utterly

LESSONS.

unfitted.   It is strange that, though people are
very particular not to select grooms who know
nothing about horses, it does not seem to occur
to them that an equally careful selection should
be made concerning the trainers of their children, and nobody chosen for that work who does
not truly understand the mysteries of child life.

But it was hardly surprising that Uncle

Charley and Aunt Eleanor should not have regard to this, for they themselves did not know that there was anything in children to understand. And when Miss Grimston arrived weighted with testimonials, they were only too glad to secure her services, and hand over Babs and Teddy at once into her keeping.

But the children did not take to Miss Grimston. They disliked her stiff, severe manner, and shrank from her grey, granite nature.

" She's not very nice," said Babs solemnly to Teddy, " and her hands is all loose bones what might rattle. I don't fink I like her much."

" Nor I don't," agreed her brother. " She won't be able to play one bit, and I know she'll scold. I wish some wild beasts would eat her all up!" he added fervently.

Babs looked very serious until the last happy suggestion.

" P'r'aps they will!" she exclaimed cheerfully, " anyhow we can hope it."

The nursery had been turned into a schoolroom, and poor Nana sent with tears in her eyes to sit in the maid's room with Wace.

" Good-morning, children," gasped Miss Grimston, breathless from her mount up the long flight of stairs.

"Good-morning," they answered gravely, from a distance. Children generally know by instinct whom it is safe to kiss.

"Come near and shake hands nicely," continued the governess.

"I don't fink I'd like to shake hands with you," said Babs, "your fingers is so bony."

Miss Grimston looked severer than ever. "You are a very rude little girl," she said sternly. But perhaps she thought it better not to press the matter. Teddy was soon settled with a copy to write, and Miss Grimston brought out a *Child's Guide to Knowledge* with which to educate Babs.

After reading over a few questions and answers several times, during which process Babs sat with a wondering look on her bright little face, Miss Grimston decided that the lesson had been sufficiently learned.

"Stand with your hands behind you, Barbara!" she said.

"Why?" asked Babs surprised. She had never done such a thing in her sensible out-of-door life before, and she did not see any reason in doing so now. Perhaps on the whole Babs was right.

" Because I tell you to, that is enough for little girls."

Babs looked puzzled for a minute and then a sudden light illuminated her face.

" Are I goin' to do 'nastics?" she said with a little laugh.

Miss Grimston took no notice of her question, but turned to the open book.

" ' My dear child, are there not many things that you would like to know?'"

" Oh yes!" screamed the little girl delightedly. " I would like to know what makes there come such a lot of colours in the water bottles, and why the crumbs jump up when we slaps the table, and —— "

" Be quiet, Barbara!" said the governess angrily.

" But you asked me!" exclaimed Babs, bewildered by the rebuke.

" You were saying your lesson remember. The answer is ' Yes '."

" ' Yes, please,' I s'pose?" interrupted the little girl.

Miss Grimston returned to the book.

" ' Pray then what is bread made of?'"

" Dough and barm," replied Babs promptly. " I've often seen cook make bread at Cloverdale.

Teddy and I used each to have a piece to
make little men with bead eyes what grew fat
in the baking."

" Silence!" cried the governess in despair,
" that is not the right answer."

" Isn't bread made of dough and barm in
London? It always is in the country, I know."

" The answer is 'flour'! What were you
thinking of, Barbara, when I read this lesson to
you?"

Babs looked doubtful for a minute. " I was
finking about what makes you have so many
more bones in your hand than other people's,"
she said candidly.

" Be quiet, Barbara! How dare you be so
rude?"

" Am I rude? I didn't know, but you is so
funny," continued the little girl, " you keep
asking questions, and when I answers them
you say, ' Be quiet'."

" You are a very naughty, pert little girl, and
I shall put you in the corner."

" What's that?" asked Babs with interest.
Hitherto she had been quite ignorant of nursery
penalties.

" Go and stand in that corner with your face
to the wall."

Babs cheerfully complied.

"What happens now?" she asked a minute afterwards.

"You will remain there until you are good."

"I'se like a cow what's in a stall," laughed Babs. "Teddy, I'se pretendin' I'se dear Flossy. We've never played this game afore."

"Be silent, Barbara!" cried Miss Grimston in the last stage of irritation. "It is not a game at all, it is a disgrace."

Babs then began to make a sort of gentle munching sound, and occasionally shook out the ends of her sash.

"That's Flossy's tail whisking," she murmured, quite content.

The exhausted governess now turned her attention to Teddy's copy-book, and to her dismay perceived a number of black lines covering the whole page.

"What is this?" she asked severely.

"You told me to cover with ink the lines that were made, and then to copy them. I like covering the lines best, so I left the letters till last."

Miss Grimston looked at Teddy. He had such a sweet, innocent face that he could not really have meant to be naughty. It did not

occur to the governess that an angel face may
be coupled with a boy's soul. And, besides,
she had already decided that Babs was the
naughty one. The little girl had been so rude
and obstinate, while Teddy seemed so gentle
and polite. So after a mild rebuke, she turned
over a new leaf, and watched for a while his
laborious attempts to copy the printed writing.

And certainly Teddy was not so actively
naughty in school-time as Babs. He was so
much less intense than his sister in all his
feelings that this was really the result of idle-
ness rather than of excessive virtue. Poor Babs
was always in trouble of some kind, and the
sad part of it was that it all came without her
meaning to be naughty at all.

"Fings so often turn out nasty," she said
wistfully to Teddy.

But this was how it happened. Miss Grimston had a strict theory that school-time must
be kept rigidly, and no irrelevant talking or
laughter allowed therein ; and Babs's nature
and habit were always to talk and generally to
laugh. She thought of so many things to say,
and her words tumbled out before she remembered it was school-time ; and also such lots of
funny things happened that she could not help

laughing at them. Miss Grimston's pen might give a scratch, or better still the slate pencil a squeal, and the little girl would break out into the merriest laughter. She really could not help it, for it was so splendidly funny when a book fell down, or Miss Grimston knocked her knuckles against the piano, or Teddy dropped his pocket-handkerchief. She had always laughed out of the fulness of her cheery little heart, and how could she be changed, all in a week, to suit Miss Grimston's fifty-year-old fads? But of course Babs did not see all this. She only knew that she was always being scolded and punished for doing what was to her the most natural thing in the world—and really how could she help it?

Bad reports of her conduct were continually being sent downstairs, and Aunt Eleanor said it was just what she expected—but Uncle Charley only laughed. Miss Grimston's battles with Babs amused him vastly.

One of the most serious bones of contention between the little girl and her governess was the weekly letter to her father or mother in India. Babs had been accustomed to printing in wild, crooked letters a few disjointed, quaintly-spelled sentences entirely out of her

own head ; and her mother was wont to laugh,
and cry, over these dear, funny little letters,
which generally ended in a lot of kisses and
scribbling, all of which Babs felt sure her
mother would understand as well as she did.
But with Miss Grimston came a new order of
things.   She insisted on proper letters written
in a large round hand, and saying such things
as she thought fit, or sometimes pencilled
underneath.   And Babs, who saw the impro-
priety of this style of correspondence, rebelled.

" If you say the fings it is your letter," she
argued one Thursday morning, while Teddy
was peacefully plodding through Miss Grimston's copy on the slate.   He was glad to be
saved the trouble of making it all up for himself.

" Do not be so troublesome, Barbara," said
the governess grimly.

" I aren't troublesome," answered Babs, "on'y
I do want to send mother a letter of my very
own."

" What do you wish to say ? " severely.

" I can't tell you, really, Miss Grimston ! "

" And why not, pray ? "

"It wouldn't be at all polite, 'cause, you see,
I want to tell mother 'bout you."

Miss Grimston's face became very sultry.

"Your mother would not read such a naughty, rude letter," she remarked sternly, and with a remarkable disregard of truth.

" Yes, she would ! " contradicted Babs, flushing with temper, " and she would like it much better'n your dirty old letters," defiantly.

" I shall not allow you to write at all, unless you behave yourself, and come at once and ink over this pencil copy which I have done for you."

Miss Grimston stooped to lift Babs on to her high chair, but the child stiffened in every limb, which is a sure sign of infant depravity, and uttered a piercing, tearless yell.

" You are an exceedingly naughty little girl," said the governess angrily, "and I shall not allow you now to write at all. I shall send a note instead to your mother to tell her how naughty you are."

Babs began to cry violently and sat screaming on the floor while Miss Grimston fulfilled her threat ; and Teddy, after the manner of children, took absolutely no notice whatever of the storm of tears.

" Cease that noise at once, Barbara," said the governess as she looked over Teddy's dull little letter.

But here again Babs had neither the power
nor the inclination to obey. It would have
been a physical impossibility for her to suddenly
swallow down all her woe.

Miss Grimston picked her up with a vicious
little shake.

" Do you hear me ? Cease crying this
moment ! " she repeated.

And Babs's spirit rose within her.

"Get away,—you—you—you beast ! " she
cried passionately.

A chill horror fell upon the room. Miss
Grimston's bony fingers relaxed their hold, and
she solemnly rang the bell for nurse.

" Put Miss Barbara to bed at once," she said
in an awful voice when Nana appeared. "And
she is to remain there in disgrace for the rest
of the day. I shall inform Captain and Mrs.
Conway of her outrageous conduct myself."

Nana was only too glad to carry her darling
away from the governess, and the dreaded
dominion of lessons ; and she hushed and
soothed the sobbing child, though she dared
not disregard the command to put Babs to
bed.

" My letter ! " wailed Babs. " I on'y wanted
to write to Mother and tell her how horrid Miss

Grimston is, an' now she'll write and tell her
I've 'rageous conduck, like Uncle Charley
and Aunt Eleanor, and nobody won't understand."

" You shall write yourself, lovey," said nurse
soothingly, " and Nana'll put it in the post, and
it'll be all right."

The thought of the letter wonderfully cheered
Babs, and the sorrows of the morning were
quite forgotten in the excitement of writing it
that afternoon.   She sat up in bed in her little
red dressing-gown, with flushed cheeks and very
bright, eager eyes.

" It shall be a very long one, and Nana, you
must tell me when I can't spell the fings kite
right."

" That I will, Miss Babs dear," said nurse
lovingly.

" Called her a beast, did she ?   Bravo ! "
laughed Uncle Charley, after Miss Grimston
had gone home in a whirlwind of righteous
wrath.   " What a lark ! "

Aunt Eleanor laughed too.

" She is an old cat, I must say ; but really
Babs is an awful child.   I shall be thankful
when Ned and Barbara come home ! "   And
then the remembrance that Teddy was in the

room, playing by himself in the back drawing-room, changed the conversation.

" Uncle Charley and Aunt Eleanor aren't a bit angry with you 'bout Miss Grimston," said Teddy cheerfully, as he had tea—a cosy tea prepared by Nana, on a little table beside Babs's bed. " They both laughed, and Uncle Charley called you a lark, and Aunt Eleanor said Miss Grimston was a cat. And uncle seemed rather glad you'd called her a beast."

" Did he really ? I fought it was dreadful naughty ! "

" But Aunt Eleanor said you were an awful child."

" I know ; that's 'cause I'm not pretty. Do you fink Mother will mind 'bout me not being pretty too ? "

" I don't know. Did you write Mother a long letter ? "

"Oh, yes, a splendid one, what told her all 'bout it."

" Barbara," said Miss Grimston sternly, on the following morning, " are you prepared to apologise for your unseemly insult of yester-day ? "

" What do you say ? Are I what ? " asked Babs, somewhat puzzled.

" Are you sorry for speaking to me as you did yesterday ? "

" Oh, yes ! " said Babs eagerly, for children never bear malice. " I are very sorry, and to-day I are kite good."

" I am glad to hear it," said the governess thawing a little, " and I hope you will never be such a wicked child again."

" Uncle Charley didn't fink it at all naughty to call you a beast," continued Babs pleasantly, " he seemed rather glad, Teddy said. P'r'aps he and Aunt Eleanor don't fink beast a rude name. I don't 'spect they can, 'cause Aunt Eleanor said you were a cat, and in course she couldn't be rude. But a cat is a beast too, isn't it ? "

Miss Grimston's face became a dull chocolate colour. It was her way of blushing. But she did not know what to say. She only felt a feeling of intense irritation against the innocent child.

" Look over your geography lesson while Teddy says his spelling," she almost hissed.

Babs looked surprised. What had made Miss Grimston angry again was a complete wonder to her. She supposed it was one of the inexplicable mysteries of the grown-up.

Babs hated geography, but the lesson had one redeeming feature. In due course Miss Grimston asked what was the capital of Cornwall, and Babs answered with a little shriek of amusement :—

"Bodmin on the Camel's back".

Teddy had been the original perpetrator of this excellent joke, but its repetition brought unfailing delight to Babs. A severe rebuke always followed in its train, but the children resignedly bore that for the sake of the wit.

Music lessons too were always a sorrow to Babs. Teddy was a musical boy, and caught things by ear, and in fact took as naturally to the piano as a young duck to water, but practising to Babs was labour and sorrow.

Miss Grimston sat beside her and occasionally rapped the fat, stupid little fingers with her spectacle-case rather sharply. A note once played wrong was always played wrong in Babs's case. She toiled through the "Blue Bells of Scotland" with the greatest effort, and invariably alighted on C instead of E for the "bonny" note.

"I'se so hot," she gasped after her sixth try for E, "mightn't I rest a bit?"

"Certainly not. Play your scales now."

The thumb-wrench, or, as it might be called, the thumb-screw, in the scales was even more exhausting, and Babs drew her breath hard in her anxiety to accomplish it.

"I writed to Mother all yesterday afternoon," began the little girl presently ; for she had no idea of secrecy. There never had been any reason for it in her happy life up till now— "And I telled her all 'bout the beast."

"Then you are extremely defiant," said Miss Grimston angrily. "I specially forbade you the privilege of writing to your parents, and I am much displeased at your daring to do so."

Babs bowed her head to the storm—but she did not quite understand what her governess was saying.

"Teddy," she said, when lessons were over, and Miss Grimston gone, "I don't fink I'll tell fings again to people what don't understand—it makes it so nasty."

"I wouldn't," answered her brother, "it's safer not."

"What makes it be safer?" asked Babs. "It never mattered at home."

"Giles and Nana were different."

"I'm glad I writed to Mother—she'll be pleased to get such a very long letter."

But the arrival of that mail in India brought a good deal of anxiety to Major and Mrs. Conway.

"Oh, my poor Babs!" cried her mother; "do look at what she says, Ned!" and then she showed him the funny little printed scrawl :—

"Der Muvver, shes dredful I cald her a beest an I wis yood cum home soon your lovin littel Babs".

"And there's such a horrid letter from that odious governess, I know she's unkind to my poor baby. Oh, Ned, do take me home to them as soon as ever you can!" And Barbara Conway covered her little daughter's letter with kisses—and when the major took it up the page was all wet.

"What does the boy's letter say?"

"Oh, just a dull schoolroom copy—not from Teddy at all, but done by that woman. But I'm sure, Ned, that things are going wrong. Oh, I do want to go home so dreadfully! It is very good of Charley and Eleanor, but they know nothing about children—and now they've got this horrid governess! Read her letter, and then burn the vile thing!"

So Major Conway read :—

" DEAR MADAM,

"I feel it my painful duty to inform you that your daughter Barbara is in so insubordinate a frame of mind, that she is unfit to write to you her periodical letter to-day ; and also that her conduct is at times so outrageous that ordinary childish penalties prove utterly inadequate.

"Yours truly,

"ELIZA GRIMSTON."

" Beast ! " exclaimed his wife. Thereby echoing her little daughter's sentiments of nearly a month ago.

# CHAPTER VI.

## RONALD'S VISIT.

TEDDY and Babs were in a state of great excitement, for Aunt Eleanor had just been into the nursery to say that an uncle of theirs, whom they had never seen, was coming to spend a few days at Onslow Square, and would bring with him his little boy who was just six years old.

" I'm so glad he's not seven ! " exclaimed Babs, " 'cause being six makes him equally between us."

" Six is rather little," said Teddy loftily from his superior standard of seven.

" Oh, no ! Teddy, it's just a splendid age ! " persisted· Babs eagerly. " What fun we shall have ! "

And the best of it all was this : Uncle Charley said Miss Grimston should take a little holiday, so that Teddy and Babs could play with their cousin Ronald all the time.

A long while before Ronald and his father

could possibly arrive, Teddy and Babs stationed
themselves at the nursery window, while Nana
held on to them behind to prevent them in
their eagerness from overbalancing themselves.

It was quite a treat being allowed to look

RONALD.

out of an open window at all, and Babs
thoroughly appreciated it.

"Look, Teddy! isn't it fun seein' into the
open carriages? That lady has a red book
on the seat opposite, and that gentleman is
crying."

7

"It's dust in his eye, I expect," suggested
Teddy.

"And, oh, look, Nana! that old lady is
peaking to the footman. Do you fink she's
asking him if the horses are tired or which is
the way home? Oh, I wish we could hear!
And there's a nice hansom walking, and the
driver has a newspaper open what he's reading
at the top. I never knew drivers read while
they was driving hansoms. But it makes a
lovely table. I'd like to be a hansom driver,
all 'cept the readin'. I don't like readin'. How
funny things look from up here! I 'spects
angels see like we do now from right up so
high. I'm so 'cited 'bout Ronald! He's sure
to be nice and play with me too, isn't he,
Teddy?"

"Yes, indeed, Miss Babs dear," interrupted
nurse, "you must all three play together nicely
—I won't have the boys leaving you alone."

"You won't want to, will you, Teddy?"
asked Babs wistfully.

"There's a cab with luggage, perhaps that's
Ronald?" suggested Teddy, who did not wish
to make any rash promises.

The excitement of the cab, even though it
did not pull up at the door, quite diverted Babs,

until she caught sight of her uncle who had
just come out of the house.

" Look ! " she cried, " there's Uncle Charley.
He's speakin' to William—an' he's rather cross
I fink. Now William has run back into the
house for something, and Uncle Charley's
tappin' his stick in a hurry. Oh, it's cigarettes !
I 'spect those were the ones what William
meant to smoke himself, only Uncle Charley
will have them. Poor William ! Oh, look !
there's another cab—and it's stopping here.
Oh ! " she screamed, " it must be Ronald ! Can
we go down now, Nana, or must we wait till
Aunt Eleanor sends up ? "

" She will send directly, lovey. Let me
brush your hair, and wash your hands and take
off your pinafore all ready."

When Teddy and Babs were ushered into
the drawing-room, they saw a tall gentleman
and a little, thin, dark boy, dressed in a kilt,
who had such a bright, laughing face that Babs
smiled too, and said : " I likes you, Ronald !
And what a funny little short thick frock you
have got on."

" That's my kilt. I'm a Scotchman, you
see."

" What's inside the rabbit ? " asked Babs,

stroking Ronald's sporran, while Teddy was talking to Aunt Eleanor and his new uncle Jack.

"Oh, Daddy!" cried Ronald, "she calls my sporran a rabbit. Isn't she funny?"

Babs never minded being laughed at; she was such a merry little soul that she always laughed too, and everything was pleasant. It was different with Teddy, he hated any one to laugh at him; but herein the little boy and girl were not very unlike big ones.

Nursery tea that night was delightful. Ronald was such a dear, jolly, little fellow, and so full of excitement about coming to London.

"I have got to see everything in London in one week," he told Babs, between his mouthfuls of bread and jam; "and Daddy has promised to take us all to the Zoo his own self,"

"Us too?" screamed Babs in ecstasies at the thought.

"Yes, of course; and to see the river."

"We've seen the river," said Teddy.

"Yes, there is such funny boats on it what puts their spouts down," added Babs.

"Too, I want to hear all the bells we sing about that say things."

"What things?" asked the little girl.

" Oh, don't you know? ' Oranges and lemons, says the bells of St. Clement's.' "

" ' I owe you five farthings, says the bells of St. Martin's,' " chimed in Babs. " I never fought somehow they was real bells."

" Of course they are," said Ronald. " What day is to-day? "

" Monday," answered Teddy.

" And we go home on Saturday. That makes it very awkward, 'cause I 'spect they only ring on Sundays."

" I never heard them," said Teddy.

" I don't fink ' oranges and lemons ' would be kite Sunday fings to say. It's a week-day game, you see," observed Babs.

" What a bother! " said Ronald. " I'll ask Daddy, he'll know all about it."

" Will he understand? " asked Babs a little anxiously.

" Understand? of course he will! He always understands things I ask him. All fathers do."

" Do they? " exclaimed Babs, brightening up again, " we didn't know."

" Our father and mother are in India," said Teddy.

" I've only got a father," said Ronald, " you're better off than me."

"I fink it's better to have only a father in London, than a Father-and-Mother-in-Inja," was Babs's opinion.

The next day Uncle Jack proposed a visit to the Zoo. And he and Uncle Charley said that they would take the three children off by themselves, which plan delighted Aunt Eleanor, who was full of other engagements of her own.

William was told to whistle two hansoms, and the children capered about in wild excitement at the prospect even of the drive.

"Who will come with me?" said Uncle Jack.

"I will, Daddy!" shouted Ronald.

"And I!" echoed Teddy and Babs in one breath.

"Won't anybody come with me?" said Uncle Charley.

Babs's face flushed. She wanted dreadfully to ride with Ronnie, but yet her loyalty to Uncle Charley interfered. Both uncles saw the struggle; but Uncle Jack lifted Ronald and Teddy into the first hansom, and then turned to do the same for Babs. Uncle Charley stood alone behind.

"I fink I'll go with you," said Babs, suddenly

turning towards him, " else you might be rather
lonely."

" Yes, I might!" said Uncle Charley, stroking
her hair more tenderly than he had ever done
before. He was rather touched by the baby
bit of self-sacrifice for his sake.

So the cabs started ; and Uncle Charley kept
looking down at the child beside him with a
new interest.

" How absurd to be pleased by such a little
thing!" he thought to himself. But a child's
affection is not a little thing, only Captain Conway did not know this.

" I'se glad I comed with you," said Babs
presently.

" Why ? " asked Uncle Charley.

" 'Cause you're my own uncle."

" So is Uncle Jack."

Captain Conway had forgotten that Major
Bruce was only related by marriage. Anyhow Babs was quite ignorant of such a dis-
tinction.

" I fink you are more owner," she decided
after a little deliberation.

" What makes you think that ? "

" Well, you see, Uncle Jack's got Ronnie
for his own little boy, and you've got me,"

she added triumphantly.   " So I must be more
yours."

" She is really rather nice," thought Uncle
Charley, but aloud he said :—

" And who does Teddy belong to ? "

" Aunt Eleanor in course."

" And don't you belong to Aunt Eleanor
too ? "

" Oh, no ! " said Babs simply ; " Aunt Eleanor
on'y likes to have pretty little girls.   But if
Ronnie is Uncle Jack's, and Teddy is Aunt
Eleanor's, I must be yours."

" And who belongs to your father and
mother ? " continued Uncle Charley.

" Oh, Father-and-Mother-in-Inja haven't got
no children.   Look, look ! " she screamed,
" we're passing Ronnie's cab ! "

And the waving of hands and hats became so
enthusiastic that it was a wonder none of the
three children tumbled out.

Uncle Charley and Babs arrived first, and
stood waiting for the others.   In getting out
of his cab Uncle Jack nearly knocked his hat
off, which was looked upon as an exquisite
joke by the children.   Ronald shouted with
laughter, and the others took their cue from
him.

" Uncle Jack's not a bit like you, is he,
Uncle Charley ? " said Babs. " 'Cause when
fings mess your hats you get very cross, but in
course you have to 'cause your hats is all so
delicate."

" Mine is pretty strong," said Uncle Jack
smiling.

"It looks older than Uncle Charley's. P'r'aps
that's what makes it stronger ? " suggested
Babs.

" The lions and tigers is all shut up tight,
isn't they ? " asked the little girl somewhat
anxiously, as they entered the Zoological
Gardens.

" Oh yes, of course ! And inside very thick
iron bars," her uncles assured her.

It was all very exciting, for none of the
children had ever seen any wild animals before ; and it was as if their best picture-books
had suddenly come to life. The elephant rather
staggered Babs as she looked up and saw the
line of his back against the sky. He seemed
to her about the size of the Imperial Institute
or Westminster Abbey.

They loved the monkeys very dearly, and
shrieked with laughter when those quaint, sad-
faced little creatures performed their accus-

tomed antics. Babs thought it would be delightful to have a little monkey of her own instead of her best doll.

"The camels is like a Sunday picture!" she exclaimed, as she saw them walking across the garden.

But the thing that delighted the children most of all was a tiny wild mouse, which had crept into one of the cages to feed on the bits of grain. It was not part of the entertainment at all, but it appealed more to the child-mind than any of the captured animals. They rushed to bring their uncles, who were enjoying their cigars outside, to see the wonderful mouse, and when at last it scuttled away, loud were their lamentations.

"What a darling mouse it was!" cried Babs.

"I would have liked it awfully to take home and put in a cage," said Ronald.

"And I should," chimed in Teddy.

Babs held Uncle Charley's hand very tightly in the lion house, but Teddy and Ronald rushed about and shrieked "Shoo!" in their shrill little voices right under the big lion's nose. But he was thinking about Africa, and looked beyond the children in doing so, just as we do when we are not thinking about the people who are speaking to us.

"The tigers is like 'normous, great, wicked, tabby cats," Babs thought; and though she did not like to own it, they frightened her rather. Teddy waxed very brave about tigers, having regard to the thick iron bars.

"They look savage," he told Ronald and Babs, "but you can frighten them if you look them in the face. If I met a tiger I should stand staring right into his eyes, and then he wouldn't touch me. I read about it in a book."

"I should run away as fast as I could, and shut my eyes tight," said truthful Babs.

"Oh, you silly!" exclaimed Teddy scornfully; "then you'd get eaten. You should look him in the face like I should."

Just then Teddy turned down a pathway alone to explore, while Ronald ran back to ask his father something, and Babs went with him. A minute later the boy who would have faced a tiger rushed out for his very life with a terrier yelping at his heels. It required Uncle Jack's prompt assistance to drive away the dog, and soothe Teddy's sudden fright.

"Why didn't you stand still and look him in the face?" asked his uncle, when calm was restored.

Teddy's cheeks grew very pink, but Babs came to the rescue.

" Dogs is different, I 'spect," she said loyally,
"and in course it's no use standing still to be
bit."

" Of course not," said Uncle Jack pleasantly.
" Let's go and buy some buns, I daresay you
are all hungry."

The buns were a charming diversion, and
Babs would insist on leaving a few crumbs
from hers in different places, " in case that dear
mouse came back ".

Another day of Ronald's visit was filled by a
still greater excitement.  Uncle Jack's father
and mother lived in a house past which a royal
procession was going, and the Queen herself,
on her way to open some great public building.
And the three children were invited to come
and spend the day with Lady Bruce, and see
the show from there.  Aunt Eleanor went too,
and to the children's sorrow laid down the law
that three of them were really too many to be
on the balcony crowding out other guests ; so
Babs was sent upstairs to see from an upper
window, and Teddy was allowed to remain
with Ronald on the drawing-room balcony.

Poor Babs felt just a little lonely when she
found herself separated from the boys.  And it
would not be nearly so interesting to see the

Queen now Ronald was not beside her ; for
Babs and Ronald had been talking a good deal
about the Queen and the part she would take
in the procession ; and they had at length
arrived at the conclusion that she would be
seated on the top of a gilt carriage with a rose-
coloured dress and a helmet on her head.

"And a hay-fork," added Babs.

" But that was Britannia, I think," said
Ronald doubtfully.

" Wasn't Britannia a queen ? " asked Babs.

" Oh, yes ! she rules the waves, you know."

" Well, queens is all alike," argued Babs
triumphantly, and Ronald did not feel quite
equal to gainsaying this statement.

And now Teddy would have all the fun with
Ronald, and Babs felt banished indeed.

" I wish my hair was golden, or something,"
she thought to herself sadly, " and then Aunt
Eleanor would like me to be downstairs. But
she doesn't now when there's visitors ! "

Fortunately Sir John Bruce's coachman's
wife and two children, one of whom was quite
a baby, were also in the room upstairs, and
Babs found much consolation in kissing the
baby and taking to the funny little mews-boy,
who touched his forehead when he spoke and

called her "miss," just like a real, big, live
groom.

"Father's carriage has gone to the show
and taken the master along of it," he told Babs.

"Is Uncle Jack's father the master?" she
asked with interest.

"Aye, that's it! Sir John and me lydy.
We calls your uncle Mr. Jack."

"Tommy, Tommy!" said his mother, a
sweet, pale-faced young woman, who looked as
if fresh air rarely blew through London mews,
"don't forget your manners, and mind you say
'miss' to the little lady."

"Yes, miss!" said Tommy instantly, hitting
his forehead with his forefinger. "My! we
'ad a busy die yesterday agettin' the carriage
all ready—miss."

Babs looked out of the window for a little—
but she could not take it all in. A big pageant
is beyond the child-mind. One regiment of
soldiers, or a village funeral, is as much of the
processional as they can grasp at once. So
Babs returned to Tommy and the baby.

"My, there's some 'orses!" was Tommy's
comment every now and then; but Babs was
quite happy sitting up on the bed and stroking
the coachman's baby's funny little downy head,

and inducing it to utter a gurgling laugh by playing bo-peep with it under the counterpane. A row of housemaids filled up the window, and they had an excellent view of everything.

But downstairs Teddy and Ronald were enjoying the gay scene much more thoroughly. Ronald, who lived with his father's regiment, was a great authority on uniforms, and he was able to tell the admiring Teddy the military standing of almost all the members of the procession. Occasionally Teddy baffled his real knowledge, but Ronnie was a sharp little fellow, and put down doubtful ones as lord lieutenants, which effectively silenced his cousin.

As the time when the Queen was expected drew near, the little boys got ready to wave both hats and handkerchiefs.

" It's lucky I had a clean pocket-handker-chief this morning," said Ronald, " 'cause it would never have done to have waved a dirty one at the Queen."

" I didn't see the crown," exclaimed Teddy, afterwards.

" I was so busy shouting and waving that I didn't see anything," said Ronald candidly. " But it was splendid, wasn't it ? "

And then there came luncheon, and Uncle

Jack fetched Babs downstairs, and the children had a dear little dinner all to themselves in a back room, over which there was no superintendence, and they could eat just what they liked.

" It was a splendid plan us having dinner in a different room to you," said Babs on their way home in the carriage.   " We did 'joy it so very much."

Her uncles both laughed.

" I expect you will all be ill to-morrow," observed Aunt Eleanor.

" Don't you like having dinner with us ? " Uncle Charley asked her.   She was sitting on his knee because the carriage was so full. And somehow since that drive to the Zoo Uncle Charley and Babs had begun to be friends.

" I'd like to have dinner with you, but I'll whisper the rest," she added cautiously, and put her mouth close to his ear.

What with the noise of the carriage and the roar of the streets her uncle could not hear a word that she said, but Babs tickled his ear so much that he was obliged to rub it.   This was a great joke to the little girl.   She went off into peals of laughter, and of course wanted to whisper again just for the fun of the thing, but Aunt Eleanor interfered.

" For goodness' sake, Charley, don't encourage the child so ! You make her so silly."

And then the grown-ups began to talk dull talk, and the children were left to themselves.

" What did you fink of the Queen, Ronnie?" asked Babs that night.

" I did not see her," answered Ronald. " What did you ? "

" I didn't see her 'cause the maids was all in the window, an' I was playing on the bed with the dearest little baby what was the coachman's."

" I looked so hard that I saw nothing," Teddy owned.

But for long afterwards the children talked of the great procession, and boasted of that day when they saw the Queen.

Then too Ronald's visit made the every-days so nice. He invented such lovely games to play in Kensington Gardens, and they were always games in which Babs was wanted.

" I like Babs to play," said Ronald to Teddy, "she makes things so jolly and laughaty."

Ronald generally preferred to be either a soldier or a horse, and it was delightful gallop-

8

ing up Queen's Gate on a blazing hot July morning, and pretending they were the three horses of a gun carriage.

On the Friday Uncle Jack went with them to the Gardens instead of Nana, and that made it much more of a treat.

" Let's have our usual battle," said Ronald, when his father was safely settled on a chair in the shade.

A large piece of paper out of Teddy's pocket was torn up into six portions and screwed up tight by the children to make cannon balls.

Ronald of course personated the Scotch army, Teddy the English, and Babs for some occult reason was the Chinese.

They charged at each other from behind three trees and for a moment the firing was brisk till loss of ammunition caused Teddy to shout :—

" The battle must stop while everybody gets their own two cannon balls again."

And then it was renewed with vigour till Uncle Jack suggested that the children really must sit down and get cool.

" I know what we'll do, Babs," said Ronald ; " you take the one end of this long piece of grass in your mouth and I'll take the other, and we'll num-num till we meet in the middle."

This proved a most successful form of entertainment.

" I can num-num faster than you, Ronnie," said Babs triumphantly.

" No, you can't," answered Ronald.

" Let's have a race," suggested Teddy, " with each a piece of grass and see who num-nums it up first."

It took quite a long time selecting three pieces of grass, and then Major Bruce was called upon to cut the ends equal with his pen-knife, and to give the word for starting. They nibbled away like three young rabbits, and Babs finished first to her great delight. Ronald came in second, and Teddy immediately lost his interest in the game.

" I don't like eating grass," he said. But it was being beaten that Teddy did not like.

" Woa, woa, steady now ! " shouted Ronald, suddenly leaping into the air. " Look, Daddy, I'm a horse ! "

" Yes, so I see."

" Too, I'm a piebald horse."

" No, Ronnie, you're not," said his father teasingly.

" Daddy, I think I'm rather a piebald horse."

" Well, whatever you are you must not run

any more.  You will be so hot and tired.  And
you are all going to a party this afternoon,
remember."

"Oh, yes!" screamed Babs.  "Let me sit
by you, Ronnie!"

"Will it be a dancing party?" asked Teddy.
"I do hate dancing parties!"

"I love them," exclaimed Babs, enthusiastically; "but I've on'y been to one."

"I like eating parties best," observed
Ronald, "and games and things just between
the eating."

His father laughed.

"You young glutton!" he said.  "I'm ashamed
of you."

"I wish you was stopping past Sunday,"
said Babs presently to Ronald, "and then you
could have gone with us to church.  But I
don't like church in London as well as at
Cloverdale."

"Why not?" asked Uncle Jack.

"Oh, 'cause I don't know 'bout all the
people.  It's so 'citing at home when Mrs.
Forrester has a new Sunday bonnet, or when
one of the farmer's families goes into mourning,
and 'specially when one of the school-children
is hit.  And 'sides, I can't understand all what

they sing in London—but at home I can guess pretty well 'bout the amens and fings."

" Do you have Bible lessons?" asked Ronald.

" Rather!" exclaimed Teddy.

" Horrid ones," chimed in Babs, " from Miss Grimston—all 'bout Adam and Eve, you know."

" That ate the apple," continued Teddy, as if quoting a piece from " The House that Jack Built ".

" An' was turned out of the square," added Babs.

" You have soon become a little Londoner," said her uncle, smiling.

" I wish I wasn't," said the child, " 'cause the country was my favourite. But I rather forget 'bout it now. It's such hundreds of weeks since we left Cloverdale."

" About eight, I suppose," said Uncle Jack ; but the children had rushed off suddenly in pursuit of a wandering pigeon.

And two months is really a very long time to a little child.

The party that afternoon was quite a big one, with a long table set out in the dining-room for tea, and conjuring afterwards in the drawing-room.

But children's parties indoors are rather a

mistake.   The boys all hung round the door as
if they would not quite let go the way of
escape, and the girls stared at each other chiefly
without speaking at all.   When they went to
see the conjuring the shutters were closed, and
the room so dark that several of the smaller
children wept, and had to be taken out and
comforted.

It was all very wonderful of course, but no
more so to the children than many of the common-place wonders with which every day is
filled.   They laughed when the conjurer pulled
yards of ribbon out of his mouth, and shrieked
with delight when he found a live rabbit inside
a little boy's pocket.   But it was the appearance of the rabbit which appealed to the youthful audience, not the little boy's face.   That
was only appreciated by one or two grown-ups.
A live rabbit in a drawing-room !   No wonder
the children were enchanted.   And they would
have been equally so if a wild mouse had run
into the room, or a common cat jumped through
the window.

"Oh, Daddy !" screamed Ronald when they
reached home, "the man got a real rabbit and
showed it us.   It was in a boy's pocket, you
know."

"It had lovely lop-ears," chimed in Babs, "and 'minded me so much of dear Spottie."

"I expect the boy did not mean us to know about the rabbit at all," said Teddy, "for he seemed quite vexed-looking when the man brought it out. I shall put one in my pocket when I get home."

"And there was a lion at the party, Uncle Jack," continued Babs. "It sat just in front of me."

"A what?" asked Major Bruce, surprised.

"A lion," answered Babs calmly, as if lions were the most customary guests at children's parties. "I saw in the darkness its mane coming over the chair I sat behind."

"It wasn't a lion!" interrupted Teddy scornfully. "It was a little girl with very thick yellow hair all loose."

"Oh, I fought it was a lion," said Babs simply, "and Ronnie did. We wondered if it belonged to the man or to Mrs. Webbe what gave the party."

"I thought it had come perhaps with the boy that had brought the rabbit," chimed in Ronald.

"I did not like the boy what sat aside you, Ronnie," said Babs solemnly. "He had such a cross face."

" Too, he was a rude boy ! He said it was a nasty tea, Daddy."

" But it wasn't really, Uncle Jack !" exclaimed the little girl eagerly. " There was only two plates of bread-and-butter with nine pieces on each, and all the rest was cakes."

" You wouldn't any of you say such a rude thing as that the tea was nasty, would you ? " asked Major Bruce.

" Oh, no ! " said the children in chorus, and then Babs added :—

" If it was, I might just say so to myself, or fink it in my mind, but I would never speak it out loud."

" That is right," said her uncle, smiling.

The following day was a very doleful one for Teddy and Babs. Uncle Jack and Ronald went away.

" Good-bye, Ronnie ! I wish you wasn't going," said Babs, with a little sob in her voice, and her big eyes brimming with tears.

Ronald had been watching his father very carefully in the hall, so as he said good-bye to Babs on the doorstep he slipped something into her hand.

" I tipped Babs my only sixpence, Daddy," he explained to his father on the journey, " like

you did William and Parker. And you know,
I like Babs almost as much as if she was a
boy."

" Yes, she is a dear little girl, Ronnie."

"Aunt Eleanor likes Teddy better'n Babs,
Daddy."

" But I think Uncle Charley likes Babs the
best."

" Do you ? Oh, I'm so glad ! 'cause that
makes it quite fair, you see."

# CHAPTER VII.

## AT THE SEA-SIDE.

THE season was over. Big station omnibuses piled up with luggage lumbered through the streets instead of smart carriages, and brown paper was beginning to veil many of the windows. The flowers on the balconies were reduced to a kind of blossoming fried parsley, and the sediment of servant-life seemed all at once to have risen to the surface. Housemaids and caretakers stood about on the doorsteps of the fast-emptying mansions ; and all the livery coats seemed packed, for every footman appeared in his shirt sleeves above ground. Altogether there was a hot, spent feeling in the air that made people suddenly long for the country, and feel that it was an impossibility to stay another day in the place where they had contentedly lived for the last four or six months. Uncle Charley and Aunt Eleanor were leaving town too, with the rest of the world, and Teddy and Babs and Nana, together with several of the servants, were all going down to a small house on the east coast. The children had never seen the sea, and of course were greatly excited at the thought of their sea-side visit. Aunt Eleanor had expressed the opinion that Cowes would have been a nicer place to have chosen than Overshore, but Uncle Charley was firm in preferring the latter, chiefly because a house-holding friend there had offered to lend him a cottage. So Aunt Eleanor was obliged to give a grumbling consent, though she sighed sadly at the prospect of passing a dull month in one of the loveliest villages in England. She cheered up a little afterwards on hearing that some people she knew had a large house near Overshore, and a continually changing house-party. Uncle Charley thought bathing and sailing and basking about in flannels would be a delightful change after the frock coats and stiff collars of London ; and it really was fully a week before he expressed himself sick of such rural pursuits.

They all arrived at Overshore on a lovely summer's evening, when the sea lay like a mirror under the sky, hardly taking the trouble to break into waves at all on the smooth shining sand. Teddy and Babs were extremely disappointed at this their first sight of the sea.

"Why doesn't it jump?" asked Babs, with a look of injured surprise on her face.

"And it's so little!" exclaimed Teddy, "only like a broadish band of water just half round the land."

"An' I don't see no shipwrecks either!" continued Babs; "our sea picture-book always had shipwrecks or icebergs, or something."

But the next morning they changed their minds when they went down to play on the shore. The sea had freshened, and was breaking in crisp little waves at their feet. And then too—best of all sea-side delights to London children—they were quickly divested not only of gloves, but of shoes and stockings also, at which their enthusiastic appreciation knew no bounds.

They rushed about on the clean soft sand, and ventured so far into the water that their clothes were all splashed. They filled their buckets with a lovely wet slop that appealed straight to Babs's tenderest feelings, and emptied them again in an aimless manner, and without doing anything but enjoy themselves in a wild, mad way, as only country-born children can after a term of penal servitude in London.

"Overshore's the splendidest, most 'citing

place in the world!" exclaimed Babs, as they were dragged in to have dinner at Uncle Charley and Aunt Eleanor's luncheon.

"Better than Cloverdale?" asked Uncle Charley.

The little girl looked puzzled.

"Not kite so splendid," she decided at length, "but I fink more 'citing. Don't you, Teddy?"

"Much," said Teddy, who was not ever consumed by the spirit of loyalty, "the sea is lots jollier than the brook."

"I had a letter from India just now," said Aunt Eleanor, "from your father, and he says we must tell you that you have a little baby sister whom they will bring home to you when they come."

Babs was delighted, but Teddy did not show much interest in the news. What could a baby sister matter to him—a boy of seven years old?

"I've fought of a lovely name for it," said Babs after a few moments' silence, "I would like it called Mrs. Brown."

Uncle Charley laughed; but Aunt Eleanor said sharply :—

"That is not a name at all".

"It is," persisted Babs, "I know it is, 'cause nurse has a sister-in-law what's called it."

" That's nonsense," said Aunt Eleanor, "it
is not a proper name for a child.    And it's very
rude to contradict."

Babs's face fell.

" I didn't contradick," she said peevishly,
" on'y I do know it."

As trouble seemed imminent Uncle Charley
came to the rescue.

" Never mind, child," he said kindly ; " there
are lots of other nicer names than that.    You
think of one."

Babs began to think so hard that she refused
a second helping of pudding.    At length a brilliant thought struck her.

" I know," she cried excitedly, " I've fought
again, and I'd like her to be called Strawberry
Jam."

" Really, Babs, how silly you are ! " exclaimed her aunt.    " Now for goodness' sake,
don't cry ! " as the child's face flushed with
suppressed feeling.    " If you do you shall go
upstairs."

Babs blinked back two big tears.    She did not
say anything owing to a large lump in her throat.

" Uncle Charley," asked Teddy suddenly,
" was King Alfred the Great in the Tenth
Hussars ? "

His uncle and aunt were greatly amused.

"Ronnie told me he was when he stayed with us, but when I said so to Miss Grimston she slapped me for—what did she say she slapped me for, Babs? I forget!"

"For telling lies and being impertinent," said the little girl glibly.

"No, Babs, it was you she slapped for being impertinent."

"Oh, yes, I remember now, 'cause I said I 'spected she was born in Alfred the Great's reign and so would be sure to know. I do fink so really, don't you, Uncle Charley? But that's the way with Miss Grimston, she never understands fings."

Uncle Charley continued to laugh.

"You gave her one in the wind there, you young rascal," he said, pulling her hair. "But I'm glad I'm not your governess."

The children both laughed at the idea of Uncle Charley's being a governess.

"I wish you were, only your hands isn't bony enough," said Babs hanging on to the sleeve of his blazer. "What fun it would be if you growed fin!" Just then a lady caller was announced, who seeing the children, begged that they might stay and speak to her.

Aunt Eleanor was instantly conscious of Babs's rumpled smock and rough hair, for she had heard that Lady Harriet West was a very particular, fastidious old lady ; so she called Teddy forward, who looked sweeter than ever in his fresh new flannels, with his fair hair curling picturesquely round his forehead. Teddy really was prettier when his hair was rough and his face a little flushed.

"Is this your little nephew? How do you do, my dear ? " said Lady Harriet, kissing the boy.

" I'm quite well, thanks," answered Teddy politely, " are you the lady who is the mother of our Mr. West who asked us to come and stay in this dear little house ? "

The old lady looked pleased and so did Aunt Eleanor.

" Yes, my dear, and I hope you will come up to the castle and play with my little grandchildren. And is that your sister ? " Babs rushed forward shaking her hair back from her eyes like a Shetland pony, and Aunt Eleanor trembled.

" P'r'aps you was born in King Alfred the Great's reign, 'cause you seem really a good bit older even than Miss Grimston," she began eagerly.

Lady Harriet looked appalled.

" Have I gived you one in the wind ? " continued the little girl anxiously, with a note of real concern in her voice.

" Have you given me what, my dear ? " asked the old lady. " I do not quite understand you."

Aunt Eleanor hastily came to the rescue, and sent the children out to play. But she was really very vexed with Babs, and directly Lady Harriet had departed her anger exploded.

" I wish you would whip that child, Charley ! She is too awful."

" Oh, I couldn't ! It is much too hot," said Captain Conway still laughing. " But I thought I should have burst when Babs came out with it. It's a mercy the old girl was a little deaf or she would have been more surprised still ! "

" It's all very well for you to laugh at it, Charley, but you spoil Babs frightfully. She is an awfully naughty child, and she grows worse and worse. My heart is always in my mouth when she is in the room. And if you won't correct her she will be a perfect little fiend by the time Ned and Barbara come home."

" Oh, nonsense ! " said Uncle Charley. " She

is great fun, and a nice little thing besides. You are rather hard on Babs, Nora."

" Hard on Babs ! " exclaimed Mrs. Conway angrily ; "how absurd you are ! I never saw such a spoiled child in my life. She ought to be whipped, or she'll soon be unbearable," she added, as she went out of the room in a temper.

Charley Conway generally did what his wife wished without troubling to think matters out for himself, but he had a sense of justice deep down underneath the thick crust of selfish artificiality which she had helped so much to harden, and this sense of justice had fluttered into movement when Babs first claimed him as her own uncle, " more owner than Uncle Jack ".

" The child did not mean to be naughty," he made up his mind, as he picked up his straw hat and strolled leisurely down on to the beach to find the unpardonable culprit.

She was playing very happily on the verge of some most interesting rock pools, which disclosed wonders before undreamed of in her inland philosophy. She did not see the approach of her uncle, so enticing was a youthful crab, and his voice calling her was her first intimation of his arrival.

" Oh, here is Uncle Charley ! " she shouted
in delight to Teddy. " Is you really going to
stay ? "

" Come here, Babs," said Uncle Charley,
throwing himself down on the sand in a most
injudicial attitude.

The little girl rushed up to him.

" I'se so glad you've come ! " she said, beaming all over.

" Your aunt says I ought to whip you," he
began.

" But in course you won't, will you, Uncle
Charley ? " interrupted Babs incredulously.

" For being so rude to Lady Harriet," he
continued.

" Was I rude ? " asked Babs, surprised.
" Why was I ? "

" You must know that it is not at all polite
to talk about giving people one in the wind."

" But you did," answered Babs reproachfully ;
" so I didn't fink it could be rude ! "

Uncle Charley looked into the open little face
and the honest brown eyes, and, being a man,
his sense of justice triumphed.

" What is often not rude for a man to say is
very rude for a little girl to," he said lamely.

" I didn't know," said Babs solemnly, " but

you isn't angry with me, is you, Uncle
Charley?"

Her face looked so quaintly anxious that
Captain Conway could not resist the temptation
of exciting still further emotions.

"Suppose I am angry, Babs, what then?"

It was a terrible supposition. The little girl
sat looking down with crimson cheeks and
quivering lips, trying not to cry, and yet over-
whelmed with grief at the consequences of her
crime.

Uncle Charley watched her with a tender
amusement.

"What then?" he repeated.

Babs thus brought to bay was obliged to speak.

"I'se so sorry!" she said brokenly, "I didn't
mean to vex you!" and her eyes could not
manage to keep in the tears any longer.

Uncle Charley kissed her hurriedly.

"There, there!" he said soothingly. "I'm
not a bit vexed."

Babs flung both arms round his neck in a
most heating embrace.

"I do love you so very much," she whispered,
and Captain Conway felt he was really growing
rather fond of this little niece of his. She was
so funny, and earnest, and dear.

"Shall we build a sand castle?" he asked, when released from Babs's strangling embrace.

A shriek of delight from the child indicated that the April shower had quite passed away, though her cheeks were still wet when Teddy came running up from the sea to help them.

SAND CASTLES.

"I wish I could cry another tear for you to taste, Teddy," said Babs, who had just made the discovery that tears and sea-water taste alike. "I've licked up the two last, and they was kite salt."

"I'll taste some sea-water instead," suggested

Teddy, "and then think of it when I cry next time."

Uncle Charley began to build the most delightful castle, but just at the most interesting part he grew rather tired of it, and went back to the house.

"That's the worst of grown-ups," said Teddy, "they get tired of things so quick."

"But it's a lovely castle!" exclaimed Babs enthusiastically; "and in course Uncle Charley was too busy to stay longer. Being a soldier makes him very busy you see."

The following morning it was decided that the children should bathe, and they were delighted at the thought beforehand. There was an interesting sense of mystery in being shut up with Nana in the funny little damp house that was called a bathing-machine, though when the horse began to draw it Babs was frightened.

"The house is running away!" she gasped.

But Nana held her fast, and even lifted her up to peep through the tiny window which showed her that it was only the land that was running away after all. It was great fun, too, undressing in such an interesting place, but when the door opened sea-wards an awful terror filled Babs's soul.

"Oh, we're right in the middle of the sea!" she screamed, clinging to Nana. "Don't put me in, don't. Please don't!"

Aunt Eleanor was bathing from the next machine, and came up to the door.

"Don't be such a silly cry-baby," she said crossly, and held out her hand to Teddy.

Now Teddy was a brave boy, and seven years old, but even he could not help catching his breath with a sobbing sort of gasp when he climbed down the steps of the machine. The sight of the shore round the corner inspired him with fresh courage, and he consented, though tremblingly, to go in with Aunt Eleanor. But nothing would induce Babs to leave the safe shelter of the machine; she sat on the step, a miserable shrinking little object, and every now and then just touched the water with the tip of her toes. Only the day before she had rushed fearlessly in when paddling from the beach, and had gone so far into the water that even Teddy suggested she might be drowned, but it was the landless view from the bathing-machine door which created the terror of bathing. Finally, persuasions and threats having equally failed, Nana redressed her, and she forgot her fears, and began to enjoy watching Teddy who was jumping about with Aunt Eleanor.

"Master Teddy! Master Teddy!" called Nana from the door, "have you got your watch with you?" Nana appeared a little flurried at not finding the precious Waterbury among Teddy's garments, and it did not seem to occur to her that his present costume afforded but scant accommodation for a watch.

"No, I haven't," shouted Teddy, "it's in one of my shoes."

After his bathing experience, Teddy lorded it over Babs more than ever. He continually referred to his courage as compared to her cowardice, and every day after the bathe the little girl firmly resolved that she really would go in to-morrow. But when to-morrow became to-day, she could not help changing her mind.

When the children had been at Overshore for nearly a fortnight a great trouble befell them.

They came in to tea as usual one evening and were surprised to find Nana in tears. Babs was specially surprised, because as she confided to Teddy afterwards, she did not know that grown-up people ever cried properly.

"Oh, my poor lambs!" sobbed Nana, nearly

smothering them with kisses. "What will you
do without me?"

"Without you, Nana?" questioned Babs.
"Where is you going?"

"I must go out to India to your mother and
the new baby sister. Her nurse has died and she
don't know where to turn, poor thing! I'm sure
I tremble at the thought of that long voyage
all over again, for I've been twice to India—
once for you. Miss Babs dear, and Master
Teddy first of all—and now your poor dear
mother wants me again for the baby. And I
would be glad to go sooner than let the child
be brought up by them heathen blacks, if it
wasn't for leaving you two darlings!"

It is a terrible sorrow in child-life when a
dear, kind nurse has to leave. Teddy and
Babs cried themselves to sleep for several
nights, and half the sunshine and gladness of
their sea-side visit was spoiled by Nana's hurried departure. The advent of the new nurse,
too, was a bitter experience to the two children who had never been separated from their
devoted old one. And, unfortunately, she was
a very severe, strict person, with whom Aunt
Eleanor was delighted.

"It was no good my speaking to the child

when you and that old Nana spoiled her so dis-
gracefully," she said to Uncle Charley, for she
had been very much annoyed about the sand
castle instead of the promised punishment—
" and I do wish you wouldn't take Babs off for
any more of those ridiculous excursions. You
make her ten times as naughty. And besides
it is silly to waste such a lot of time playing
with a mere baby when there is plenty of golf
and tennis up at the Castle. I am surprised at
your caring to do so!"

" So am I!" said Uncle Charley; "but it is
a fact, nevertheless."

" Oh! I wish Nana had stayed till we wented
back to London," sighed Babs, "'cause we
don't want to do such a lot of naughty fings
there. And it was so lovely getting our clothes
all splashed afore."

For the new nurse had been very cross indeed when Babs came in with her frock and
petticoats all wet from paddling, and had cruelly
forbidden a repetition of that most entrancing
exercise, in addition to dry bread for tea, and a
dull, doleful half-hour in the corner previously.
Just when Teddy was out catching shrimps,
too, or at least trying to catch them in a very
weak little green net which had been purchased

at Overshore's one toy shop with Teddy's long-saved pennies.

Neither was Teddy exempt from nurse's discipline, as he was from Aunt Eleanor's. She offended him mortally by insisting on washing his face herself, and in that peculiar unyielding manner which strict nurses are wont to adopt.

" She washes just as if my face was quite flat," said the little boy wrathfully, rubbing his nose.

" I know," said Babs meaningly, " that horrid round and round way, like as if we was a plate. And the soap always gets in my eyes. But I fink she hurts more with the towel after."

But all the disagreeable nurses in the world could not quite destroy the delight of sea-side life. At night when the room was dark a sense of desolation would come over the children in dear Nana's departure, but in the morning when the sun shone and the sea danced things seemed quite different. Babs would remind Teddy that Nana would soon come back, bringing with her both father and mother, as well as the new baby sister, and how could anybody cry or fret while those lovely sands, smoothed fresh every night by the sea, were waiting for the children to dig on them ; while no end of beautiful pieces of seaweed were washed up on purpose for their play, to say nothing of the excitement of an occasional star-fish or crab which had been left behind by the ebbing tide. The shore too was such a splendid place for pretending, it was so like a desert island, where the Swiss Family Robinson could be enacted, or where they could have encounters with savages, or wild beasts.

Sometimes they played with other children, too. A very quaint, bunchy baby was stolidly digging a little hole one day, and Babs thought it would be a very useful addition to their pretending plays.

" Shall I speak to it ? " she asked Teddy.

" Is it a boy or a girl ? " Teddy wondered.

" I'll ask it," said Babs.

The fat baby paused in its work as the little girl approached, and endeavoured to reinstate the sailor hat which was hanging down behind its back, apparently fastened by a mixture of elastic and hair.

" Which are you—a boy or a girl ? " asked Babs, coming straight to the point.

" I'm a mon," said the fat baby solemnly, and its tone admitted of no further observation on that score.

"Will you play with us?" suggested Babs meekly.

"No piggy?" remarked the baby, irrelevantly.

"It called me a pig!" said Babs to Teddy in amazement.

But the baby's nurse explained :—

"He has been frightened by a pig, miss".

"We haven't got a piggy," said Babs, "we are pretendin' we're cast on a desert island, where there's black people."

"No piggy?" repeated the baby.

"Oh, no! on'y a few lions and tigers. A very few, and not at all savage," she added hurriedly, as the fat, round face clouded over.

"On'y yions and tigers, no piggy!" said the baby, apparently satisfied.

"Come on," shouted Teddy, "we must dig a place to sleep in to-night."

Babs seized the baby's hand, but instead of following her, he sat down rather heavily and quite unintentionally on the sand.

"I sit down!" he observed, with a very pink face, which was evident.

"He's too little to play proper pretendin'," said Teddy scornfully. "Come on, Babs!"

" Oh, dear, dear, vat a pity !" remarked the
baby.

So Teddy and Babs finished their game
alone, while the baby continued his digging,
occasionally looking round anxiously, and
assuring himself by the repeated observation :—

" No piggy fighten Baba !"

On the way up from the sands, nurse walked
with the baby's nurse, and Teddy and Babs
each held one of its fat little hands.

Babs assumed a squealing tone of voice in
addressing it, to indicate its supreme youth as
compared with her own five-year-old maturity,
and Teddy talked in the peculiar style usually
adopted towards a kitten.

" Look, little Baba, at the pretty moo-cows,"
piped Babs in a singularly shrill voice.

" They give the nice milk for Baba's tea,"
continued Teddy condescendingly.

" No old moo-cows feed Baba," said the baby
in solemn, deep tones.   " Nana give Baba nice
tea."

Babs instantly began to argue, only happily
just then the children's and the baby's ways
diverged, and a quarrel was averted.

For Teddy and Babs had been invited to

have tea at the old farm-house, and a lovely
time they had, eating shrimps out of little
china mugs, and drinking wonderful frothy milk
fresh from the very cows that the baby on the
beach had scorned. Then there was rich red
jam, and no nurse present to intimate that they
had had enough after they had only just begun.

"Did you enjoy yourselves?" asked Uncle
Charley when they reached home.

"Oh, it was splendid!" screamed the children, "and such a beautiful tea!"

"Jam and shrimps——" began Teddy.

"And ordinary cow's milk!" chimed in Babs.
And the children could not imagine what made
Uncle Charley suddenly laugh.

"It's the way with grown-ups," said Teddy
afterwards, "they often laugh at things that
aren't a bit funny."

"It was ordinary cow's milk," persisted Babs,
"'cause I asked Mrs. Grimble specially when
it frothed so much."

"Uncle Charley nearly always laughs when
we speak," said Teddy.

"Well, I loves him much better'n Aunt
Eleanor what never does. I likes laughing,"
and Babs beamed all over, "even when I don't
kite understand what is funny."

"I don't like things I can't understand," said the little boy.

Unfortunately holidays will come to an end, and summer too, for the matter of that. So the sad day dawned on which the children had to leave Overshore with all its joys and sunshine for a long, dreary winter in the little London nursery.

"It is years since we came," observed Babs, when the sea was out of sight, "but we only seem to have been here 'bout two days."

In reality they had been at Overshore just six weeks.

## CHAPTER VIII.

### THE BOGEY-OWL.

THIS was how the bogey-owl came into existence. The new nurse was very strict and disagreeable, and she told Babs most unpleasantly
one morning during her rather refractory ablutions that the policeman would come and take
her, together with all other naughty little girls,
to prison. But Babs, being a very sensible
little person, wished this suggestion authorita-
tively confirmed before she really believed it.
She had known the village policeman at Cloverdale as an intimate friend during the whole of
her life, and consequently was not alarmed at
just a blue coat and bright buttons. So, thinking it well to be on the safe side, she resolved
that she would ask a policeman for herself on
the first possible opportunity.

When nurse and the children were out
walking one day, Babs coolly accosted the
first policeman she saw, and asked simply :—

" Do you really fetch to prison all the little

girls what splash over the sides of their bath ?"

The policeman was a good-hearted man, and moreover he had a little girl of his own at home with brown eyes very like Babs, so he smiled kindly and answered :—

" No, little missy, that's only a silly tale to frighten you. The police are always ready to take care of little children and see as nobody hurts 'em. We only take bad grown-up people to prison."

Before Babs could reply, nurse dragged her away in great anger, but the little girl kissed her hand to the policeman and shouted, " Good-bye, nice policeman !" in defiance of local authority. She spent a dreary afternoon shut up in the night-nursery in consequence, but the policeman threat was finally exploded.

" I fink nurse will go to prison for her next place," suggested Babs to Teddy, " for she is grown-up and bad."

"Very bad," said Teddy, looking at his fingers which had been recently slapped.

So it came about that nurse made up for the loss of the policeman by telling the children that the bogey-owl would get them if they did not behave themselves. And this intangible horror was beyond their power to dispel. Indeed it took such a hold of them, and they thought and talked so much of the mysterious creature, that their lives after sunset became a burden, and every dark corner a possible habitation for the bogey-owl. And yet there was a great fascination in talking about it in the daylight. Only the worst of it was their talks would come back to them after the gas was put out, and increase their original fear tenfold.

" Let's talk about the bogey-owl," said Teddy one cold, foggy afternoon in November. Babs gave a little shiver, but she really enjoyed the talks in a grim way at the time.

"What do you fink it's like ? " she asked Teddy for about the hundredth time.

" Just like the picture of 'Pollyon in the *Pilgrim's Progress* that Grannie showed us on Sundays at Cloverdale, only with an owl's face and glaring eyes."

" How awful ! " whispered Babs. " I fought it was behind nurse's bed last night."

"It might be," assented Teddy gloomily, " for it must be somewhere in the house, you see, or else how could it get us so quickly as nurse says ? "

" What does it eat, do you fink, Teddy ? "

"Children, I expect. It has long bony fingers."

" Like Miss Grimston's ? "

" And it would claw you and tear you all up in pieces."

" Oh-h-h ! " gasped Babs. " I fink it is often in the bath-room at nights. I always shut my eyes tight and rush past the door. I wish the bath-room door was never a bit open."

" Sometimes it's in the chimney in my room," continued Teddy. " I hear it roaring ; but I cover my head tight with the bed-clothes."

" An' I do ; but it makes it very hot. I hate going to bed now. And nurse won't leave the gas turned on even never such a little bit."

" I wish we were back at Cloverdale."

" And I do, where there were no horrid bogey-owls, nor dreadful frightening creatures what come out at night."

" The bogey-owl never came out at all till Nana went away."

" Don't you fink it might die sometime, or be caught in a trap and killed dead ? "

" No, I don't," answered Teddy discouragingly. " I expect it'll live to be hundreds and hundreds of years old ! "

But yet though the children were so horribly frightened of this imaginary horror they talked about it more and more each day, and consequently it became more terribly real. But after the manner of children they never mentioned it to any one grown up, and even nurse herself had no idea of what a hold it had taken of their minds.

One night contrary to their usual rule they continued their conversation concerning the bogey-owl after tea, and when bed-time came Babs felt she really dared not be left alone in the dark night-nursery. She cried while being undressed, and was sharply reprimanded by nurse in the process. Teddy was so much less excitable by nature than Babs that he was able generally to put on one side the haunting fears of darkness, and fall quickly asleep under the sheltering protection of the bed-clothes. Babs had a little cold that evening, and was rather fretful and feverish, but nurse had no consideration for such foibles. She mentioned something about a dose of senna, which dried Babs's tears instantly, and induced her to go quietly to bed, rather than have to swallow such a nauseous mixture.

But when the gas was put out, Babs could

not help thinking of the bogey-owl.   She was
afraid to open her eyes lest she might see the
dreadful apparition, and she lay panting under
the bed-clothes in a perfect frenzy of terror.
The more she thought about it the more certain she was that it was in the room.   And at

THE BOGEY-OWL.

last, reckless of all consequences, she shouted
aloud for nurse, even though her coming would
involve certain scolding and probable punishment.   But nurse had gone downstairs to share
in the aftermath of a dinner-party, which Captain and Mrs. Conway were giving that night.
She had no patience with children who did not

go to sleep properly ; in fact the children she was nurse to were always made to do so. And Babs called in vain.

The darkness, the aloneness, and the imagined presence of the bogey-owl, were too much for the little girl in her frightened and excited condition. With a shriek of terror she flew out of bed, on to the landing, and down the stairs, with the cruel conviction that the bogey-owl was pursuing her, straight into the brightly-lighted drawing-room where the dinner-party guests were all assembled.

Uncle Charley and Aunt Eleanor were immensely surprised.

"Good gracious, what's the matter ?" asked the former, catching Babs in his arms.

But children rarely tell what is the matter, so Babs only burst into a torrent of tears, and clung to him with all her baby might. Aunt Eleanor quickly rang the bell, and awful indeed was nurse's countenance when summoned to remove Babs.

Surely this was trouble indeed. To be borne back to bed in deepest disgrace, and with such sundry shakes as expressed nurse's displeasure, to say nothing of the threatened penalties for the morrow, which, however, frightened Babs

far less than immediate desertion. And nurse
knew better than to leave her again. She saw
that the child was desperate, and so she did her
duty, though she inwardly vowed vengeance all
the time.

Aunt Eleanor, too, was very vexed.

" It looks as if we ill-used the child," she
complained to her husband, "and on the night
of a party, too! I saw that horrid young
Atherstone looking at me as if he thought I
ought to be prosecuted by that cruelty to children thing ! "

" Did you find out what was the matter after
all ? "

" There was nothing really the matter, only
the child was bilious, nurse says. She gave
her a good dose this morning, and has kept her
in bed."

" As a prevention or a cure ? " asked Uncle
Charley drily.

" A little of both, I expect," said Aunt
Eleanor candidly.

" I don't believe it was biliousness at all,"
continued Captain Conway. " That is a piece
of nursery conventionality. There must have
been something the matter to bring the child
downstairs in such a fright."

" What nonsense, Charley! You know nothing at all about children's ways, and it is no
use your interfering in the nursery. The new
nurse is a most competent person."

Aunt Eleanor was growing rather jealous of
her husband's interest in Babs.

" I doubt that statement somewhat," persisted Uncle Charley, " and I should like to
know what frightened the poor little thing so
much."

" You are getting perfectly infatuated about
that child!" said Aunt Eleanor angrily, " and
such an ordinary, ugly, little creature, too. I
can't understand you, Charley!"

Captain Conway glanced curiously at his wife
—at the beautiful, graceful woman who looked
so lovable—and he felt a sudden sickening want
in her, a jarring of his sensibilities at her harsh
words and vulgar thoughts.

" We are in the place of Babs's father and
mother," he said slowly. " I don't think mothers
talk like that. Mine never did." And then he
went out of the room, and straight upstairs into
the night-nursery.

Poor Babs had rebelled against the hideous
spoonful of black, sticky medicine with which
nurse greeted her on waking, and also begged

to be allowed to get up as usual. But nurse
was as adamant.

" Little girls who don't go properly to sleep,
but rampage about the house, must be very
far from well, and treated accordin'," she said
severely.

" I are kite well to-day ! " pleaded Babs.

" It is my opinion you'd be all the better for
a good whipping," observed nurse grimly, and
Babs thought it prudent to drop the conversation.

Teddy, too, was not very sympathetic. He
thought it silly to be quite so frightened of the
bogey-owl, and could not imagine how Babs
could rush down in the middle of a party
with her nightgown on. Besides, what was
the good ?

" You should have seen whereabouts the
bogey-owl really was," he said, in the bravery
that is born of daylight, "and then we might
have set a trap."

" I was 'fraid to look," Babs confessed.

" Are you sure it was in the room ? "

" Kite sure, certain. But oh ! don't let's
keep on talking 'bout it, 'cause night'll come
soon, and then I shall fink it all over again."

So when Uncle Charley came in Babs was a

very sad little person indeed. She cheered up as he sat down beside her, and they really had a most comforting talk.

" Tell me, Babs," asked her uncle presently. " what frightened you so much last night? "

Babs shook her head.

" Whisper it," coaxed Uncle Charley.

But for long Babs would not be persuaded.

" I shan't be angry, little one ! "

There was a new sound now in Uncle Charley's voice when he spoke to Babs, and at last it won the child's confidence.

She would only whisper it with her mouth so close to his ear as to produce nothing but a buzzing sound, but he succeeded in catching the word "owl".

" There is no owl here," he said at a venture.

Babs nodded her head.

" There really isn't," he assured her. " Owls never come into houses."

" Not any kind of owl? " asked Babs, hope mingling with anxiety.

" No kind at all. And they would not come inside any house, even if there were. except very old tumble-down ruins. And where there are any owls they only fly out at

nights because they are so frightened themselves."

Uncle Charley's comfort lacked tact in his
zeal for truth.

"What a pity!" exclaimed Babs, "'cause it's
in the night that I'm so frightened, and that
doesn't help a bit."

Captain Conway hastened to mend his mistake, and talked long and cheerily to his little
niece.   So fear of the bogey-owl was almost
dispelled.   It settled down into only an unpleasant back-thought instead of an ever-present
terror; "because," as Teddy said, "it wasn't
nearly so frightening flying about out of doors
as it was when it lived in the bath-room or
behind nurse's bed".

There were other fears besides that lay heavy
on the children's souls, but those perhaps no
one could have helped.   Babs was always afraid
lest wild beasts should be lurking on the back
stairs, and rush out at her through the men-
servants' door in the hall, or the housemaids'
one on the second landing, and Teddy was
afraid of some of the things he heard Uncle
Charley and Aunt Eleanor talking about when
he was downstairs, especially of "consols,"
which conveyed an inexplicable horror to the

child-mind. He used to talk to Babs about these mysteries and enlarge upon them until his little sister shook in her ankle-strap shoes, but there was a gruesome pleasure in doing so which the children both enjoyed.

"Old Mr. Fenton came to call to-day," announced Teddy, after one of his drawing-room visits from which Babs was generally excluded, "and he was telling Uncle Charley again about the 'Consols'."

The children had come to the conclusion that the Consols were a wicked family of old Romans who lived in the city, and this opinion was founded partly on their own imagination, and partly on Miss Grimston's description of consuls in the Roman history lesson.

"How was they to-day?" asked Babs. "As bad as ever?"

"Worse," said Teddy, "and they are going downer and downer."

"Like Giles used to say the gamekeeper's son was going. You remember, Teddy, he always finished up 'bout him with 'straight down to ruin'."

"But all the Consols seem bad, while it was only the gamekeeper's son that was."

"Let's talk about what we pretend they do," said Babs.

"They poach, of course," began Teddy, who
was a squire's son.

"And they cut good people up in slices," continued Babs, her eyes dilating with horror.

"And eat children."

"Oh, yes! Like the ogres in the fairy
book."

"And fire guns close to your ears."

"On purpose!" put in Babs.

"Of course on purpose.   Let's pretend they
are coming here to dinner."

But the talk was getting a little too realistic
for Babs's peace of mind.

"No, don't let's pretend they are coming
here, Teddy, it makes me so frightened.   Let's
pretend they are going to Miss Grimston's
house."

"Oh, yes.   Big old Mr. Consol has glaring
eyes and black whiskers, and great teeth, and
one day he went out to find a good person to
eat," began Teddy, whose imagination was fer-
tile in the creation of horrors.

"Miss Grimston wouldn't be good enough,"
interrupted Babs eagerly.   "But it would be
rather fun if he eated her, Teddy.   Let's make
him want only to eat bad people to-day."

"Oh, no!" argued Teddy, "else he wouldn't

be at all frightening. It wouldn't be wicked to eat only bad people, you see."

" Well, who can he eat ? "

" I know. Uncle Jack and Ronnie."

Here Babs burst into such a scream of anguish that nurse interfered.

" Now, Master Teddy, what have you been frightening Miss Babs about again ? I won't have such nonsense, and if there's any more of it, I'll buy a birch rod, and you shall feel what that is like," she continued wrathfully. Teddy became very sulky.

" I won't talk to you no more," he murmured in an offended tone to Babs ; "you are such a cry-baby, and then everything is spoiled. You never used to be so stupid."

" I wasn't so frightened afore," said the little girl humbly.

" Cry-baby!" muttered Teddy ; " I won't play with you ever again."

So Babs was left alone, sitting sorrowfully on a little bench by the fire-place, while Teddy fetched out his soldiers, and pretended a most important battle on the ottoman.

Her little mind and heart seemed all upside down, and yet she could not discern what was really the matter ; only that things were dark

and sad and miserable, and every day **grew**
worse instead of better.

The big tears rolled down her cheeks and she
caught her breath in the attempted suppression
of heavy sobs.

" Now, Miss Babs," said nurse sharply, "give
over crying this moment, or I shall shut you up
in the night-nursery."

This only made matters worse, so Babs was
promptly removed into the penal settlement, and
left there until she had learned how to behave
herself.

She climbed up on to a chair, and looked
sadly out of the window over the top of the
mews.

She was not nearly as happy and merry now
as she used to be. Constant snubbings were beginning to dim the brightness of her child-nature,
and the still stronger element of fear which had
crept into her life cast a black shadow across
many of the once-cheerful every-days.

Happily before the little girl had been alone
for very much longer, a sandy cat appeared
upon the stable roof. A beautiful, entertaining
animal which appealed at once to Babs, and
filled her barren little soul with a new and immediate interest.

She tapped the window and the cat looked up ; clearly it was a most sociable creature.

Afterwards when she was fetched out to tea, Babs exclaimed quite cheerily : —

" There's a lovely cat on the roof under the night-nursery window ".

" What sort of a cat ? " asked Teddy, still a little coldly. For Teddy never could get over things all in a minute like Babs did.

" A yellow cat what 'minded me very much of that splendid mouser in the stable at home. I like yellow cats, they don't bite as much as other colours."

" Why not ? " shortly. Teddy could not make long pleasant remarks yet.

" They haven't so many tongues," continued Babs.

" They've just the same," remarked Teddy. " No cats have more'n one tongue."

" Yes, they have," said Babs querulously.

" No more talking," interrupted nurse, " if you will quarrel you shall eat your meals in silence. Another word and you'll go straight into the corner," she added warningly, as Babs looked inclined to speak. Teddy began to eat his bread and jam very hurriedly, for he was afraid of being suddenly bereft of it as a

11

punishment, but Babs was never thus worldly-wise.   Her slice seemed to give her a choky feeling, so she drank her milk up first instead.

"What are you most frightened of in the world?" Teddy asked Babs a few days after, when things had really been very unpleasant in the nursery.

"The bogey-owl in course," answered the little girl promptly, "and a good deal of the Consols."

"Are you at all frightened of nurse?" suggested Teddy ; "she's so dreadful cross."

"Oh, no!" exclaimed Babs, amazed.   "How could I be?   She on'y scolds and puts in the corner or night-nursery, and sometimes slaps. I couldn't be frightened of fings like her and Miss Grimston.   Are you?"

"I'm rather afraid of being whipped if it hurts," said Teddy slowly.

"But that's just real and over," answered Babs philosophically.   "But the bogey-owl is so dreadful when you fink about it, and it seems hanging round outside ready to pounce, you know."

"I'm most frightened of real things," decided Teddy, who was smarting from a recent encounter with nurse's new rod.

"Oh, I aren't! The fings we pretend are much more frightening, I fink. I don't mind Miss Grimston's slaps a bit, 'cept just that minute. They're more disagreeable than frightenin'."

" I mind that beastly birch rod that nurse has bought, and I hate her," growled Teddy.

" Then I will hate her too," agreed Babs pleasantly, " 'cause she's been so nasty to you to-day."

It never seemed to occur to Babs that she should hate nurse for the long hours of punishment which she herself had been obliged to endure since dear Nana departed for that bourne which the children always spoke of as " Father-and-Mother-in-Inja ".

# CHAPTER IX.

## BABS IN TROUBLE.

It all came of so much pretending. But then it was simply impossible for the children not to pretend. It would have been so dull to have lived their child lives only as the little Conways, when they might be pretending that they were such exciting things as soldiers or savages, cabhorses or mice. And this particular pretence which caused all the trouble was one of Babs's. Teddy was always pretending that he was a policeman, and consequently Babs wanted to be one too. But Teddy was firm on this point; he was the policeman, and Babs must think of something original for herself.

"There might be more'n one p'liceman in London!" she whimpered.

"No, there mightn't," said Teddy sharply; so Babs had to content herself with being in imagination a postman, which seemed the next best thing.

And of course a postman involved letters

There were the Indian letters which Babs zealously saved, but they did not make nearly enough.

Babs begged her uncle and aunt to give her any old letters to play with, and then she induced Martha, the second housemaid, to buy her a pot of gum, with which she and Teddy spent some delightful afternoons pasting up the old envelopes to look almost as good as new. And as they were finished one by one they were safely hidden away out of sight of nurse's sharp eyes down in the most secret depths of the old toy-box.

"The postman drops a letter in at every house," said the little girl, "but then, you see, Teddy, nurse would find it out and spoil it all. I fink I had better take the letters out, but only pretend to drop them into the houses."

So every day she started out on her walk with the packet of letters clasped fast in her fat little hand, and once or twice when nurse was well on in front Babs ran up the steps of a house and rang the servants' bell, but she only pretended to drop a letter in. She could not bring herself to part with any of the beoved treasures yet. But after a while this part of the proceedings became a little stale.

" I are a real postman," she explained to
Teddy, " and in course I must leave real letters
at the houses."

" It's no good leaving these old letters if you
are a real postman," said Teddy, " because
you see they all belong to this one house."

This was a most distressing conclusion.

" S'pose," she asked her uncle at lunch
that day, " s'pose a postman dropped the
letters at the wrong houses. What would
happen ? "

" He would be packed off about his business
pretty quickly," said Captain Conway, " for he
would not be fit to be a postman."

" You are kite right, Teddy," said Babs
afterwards in the nursery. " You see if I drop
these letters at other houses I'll be packed off
'bout my business pretty quick, 'cause I would
not be fit to be a postman."

" Don't bother so ! " exclaimed Teddy, who
was rather cross. And besides he was a policeman and had no time for thinking about letters.

So Babs was left to herself and the responsibility of her unfulfilled duties lay heavily upon
her baby soul. At last a brilliant thought
struck her. She caught sight of the post-box
in the hall nearly full of nice, clean, new letters

"I MIGHT POST ONE OF THOSE."

which Uncle Charley and Aunt Eleanor had just written.

" I might post one of those," she thought gleefully, "there's such a lot that I could take just one out, like we used to the birds' eggs, so that it shouldn't matter. Now I are fit to be a postman," she murmured with a glad little laugh, as she ran upstairs with one of the new letters in her hand.

Teddy was out driving with Aunt Eleanor, so it had to be hidden away without his seeing it.

On the following day all went well. Babs was able to lag behind nurse and Teddy out walking, and to drop the new letter, which she had carried in the packet of old ones, right into the letter-box of a strange house. And again that evening she succeeded in taking another letter out of the post-box in the hall.

This exciting programme was kept up for several days, for every night on her way upstairs she peeped into the box, and if there were plenty of letters she took out one, but if there were only two or three she conscientiously refrained. "Giles only let us take one egg if there was three left," she argued to herself, and had no further misgivings on the subject.

But at last a dreadful thing happened. It
was only a cold in her head when Babs awoke
one morning, but the consequences were terrible.
Nurse would not let her go out in the first place,
and there was the letter which she had taken
out of the box on the preceding night still unposted. She knew that it would be naughty to
keep the letter. Posting, to Babs's mind, was
just dropping it into any house that she could
manage, but she felt the importance of this
posting most thoroughly. Downstairs there
was a good deal of wonder and annoyance
about invitations unanswered or delayed, and
one or two more important letters unacknow-
ledged, but Babs heard nothing of all this.

"Does it matter very dreadful," she asked
Teddy, "if letters is sometimes a day late?"

"Oh, no," said her brother carelessly; "I
heard Aunt Eleanor say that they are often
stopped for a little in the post. But don't begin
bothering again about letters. Why can't you
be a soldier or a cab-driver instead?"

"I are a postman," said Babs gloomily. And
it was clear that Teddy could not be approached
on the subject again.

The next day Babs's cold was worse, and after
lessons nurse and Teddy went out again without

her. This was really serious. There was that letter still unposted, and Babs's conscience gave her no peace.

" S'pose a postman kept a letter in his own house for a long time," she propounded to Miss Grimston in the middle of a spelling lesson, " what would happen ? "

" He would be sent to prison as a thief," answered the governess ; " but now, no more talking, Barbara, go on with your lesson."

The horror of this information lay like lead on the child's spirits.

" It's awful wicked to keep that letter," she decided, as she sat alone in the nursery when the others were out ; " if I do I'll be sent to prison as a fief."

And then an heroic resolve came into Babs's mind. She must do her duty as a postman even at the awful risk of nurse's displeasure. She would go out and drop it into a house that very minute in spite of her cold. How lucky it was that the clean clothes had just returned from the wash requiring Martha's presence downstairs. For Martha had been left in charge of Babs during nurse's absence.

Seizing her hat, for she could not put on either her own boots or coat, she flew downstairs with the precious letter, and out at the front door unmolested.    She stopped her flight on the causeway.

" Postmen don't never run," she murmured, and was walking briskly round the corner when she came right up against Aunt Eleanor.

" Good gracious ! what is the meaning of this ! " cried her aunt, dragging her indoors, and just then nurse arrived home again with Teddy.

A great storm of scolding seemed to surge round Babs's head.

" It's my letter ; I was 'bliged to take it ! " she gasped.

Nurse gave her an angry little shake, and Aunt Eleanor snatched the letter out of the child's hand.    She could hardly believe her senses.    There was the letter her husband had written two days ago enclosing a cheque, the receipt of which they had been anxiously awaiting.

" Perhaps Charley will believe me now about Babs ! " was her first thought, and an ugly feeling of triumph rose within her, as she rushed into the smoke-room to tell her husband the story of Babs's black crime.

And  Uncle  Charley  lost  his  temper.    He

had been terribly worried about the apparent disappearance of his cheque, and to be suddenly told that the child had taken it out of his private letter-box, and, having kept it for a couple of days, had been caught by chance as she was stealing out with it on a mysterious mission of her own, was enough to make him very angry indeed.

"I never heard of such a thing!" he exclaimed. "How dare she tamper with my letters!"

Aunt Eleanor fetched Babs in haste.

"Where did you get this from?" her uncle asked sternly.

"I took it out of the letter-box. I have tooked one every day!" answered Babs, bewildered. And then she said something about a postman, but nobody understood.

Uncle Charley and Aunt Eleanor talked in such loud voices, and there seemed such a noise and confusion to the child that explanation was simply hopeless.

"This account for all the delays and bother we have had just lately!" said Aunt Eleanor; "and then creeping out of doors with this letter when she knew she had to stay in with her cold! I never heard of a child's being so sly and wicked!"

" I am as much surprised as I am displeased!" And Uncle Charley spoke in an
awful voice. He was really very much annoyed ;
and to deliberately take letters out of a letter-
box and keep them was a serious offence indeed,
to say nothing of the remarkable expedition out
of doors, and all alone, by which Babs's sin had
been discovered.

" How dare you touch my letters?" he repeated. " But I will put a stop to this kind of
thing once and for all."

And then Uncle Charley gave Babs two or
three taps on each of her fat little hands.
Surely this was serious trouble, and poor Babs
cried bitterly. It was all so dreadful and
frightening, and Uncle Charley angry was
so much more awful than anybody else in the
world.

" Oh, Teddy," she wailed, when her brother
peeped into the night-nursery whither she had
been borne in dire disgrace, " I meant to be
such a good postman and take the letters kite
right! Why did it all turn out so dreadful
naughty? I don't understand!"

" Did Uncle Charley whip you hard?" asked
Teddy, who was hungry with curiosity concerning the scene in the smoke-room.

The remembrance filled Babs with such woe that Teddy could get nothing out of her, and then nurse came in and banished Teddy instantly from the degrading atmosphere of Babs's presence.

" Naughty, wicked little girls who steal are not fit to speak to other children," she said sharply, as she shut the door.

But going out of doors on a winter's afternoon with a bad cold and no coat on, brought about more mischief still.

Babs coughed all night, and awoke with feverish hands and a pain in her chest. The doctor was sent for and kept her in bed all day with hot poultices on and lots of nasty medicine to drink. Babs thought in her hot little head that it was all somehow part of Uncle Charley's anger, but she was tired after the naughtiness and kept falling into restless sleep.

And downstairs Uncle Charley was wretched about her. His anger had quickly evaporated, and he felt as guilty about those harmless slaps as if her severe cold were all owing to them.

Aunt Eleanor's continual talk of Babs's offence irritated him dreadfully too. She was so glad to have proved to her husband that his little niece's naughtiness was of a nature that no one

really could overlook ; and he had begun to
feel sure that there must have been a big mistake somewhere.   For the more he thought of
it afterwards, the more certain he was that such
a baby could not have been such a criminal.

" I didn't understand, I really didn't ! " cried
Babs as he went up to see her in bed.

" Perhaps it is Uncle Charley that didn't
understand," he said tenderly, stooping down to
kiss her.

Babs instantly recognised the change in his
tone, though she had no idea of what he was
talking.

" Have you forgiven me ? " she asked with a
glad ring in her hoarse little voice.

" Of course I have ; and why isn't Teddy
here to play with you ?   Nurse," he called, as
he heard her outside, " why is not Master
Teddy amusing Miss Babs ?   I found her quite
alone when I came up."

" I thought you were displeased with Miss
Babs, sir, and wished her kept in disgrace,"
said nurse.

" What nonsense ! " exclaimed Uncle Charley
angrily, " and twenty-four hours afterwards
too.   It's my opinion the child will be ill from
mope.   Mind there is no more of it ! " he

exclaimed sharply, as nurse departed with her nose in the air.

" I love you, Uncle Charley," whispered Babs, a very gentle little Babs just then, and she laid her cheek confidingly on his hand. " And I promise I'll be kite good now ! "

" That's right," said Uncle Charley, kissing her. He spoke cheerily owing to an unaccountable sad feeling which had swept over him as he sat beside his little niece's bed, and he wished he had not been so angry with her the day before.

" She is so little ! " he thought pityingly, " and so completely in our power that we ought to be very good to her."

The chivalry of the man had been ignited by this little spark of humanity, and manlike he hastened to hide it with cheerful commonplaces.

" Shall we play Old Maids ? " he suggested, calling for Teddy to join them.

Oh, then they had a delightful time ! Babs sitting up in bed with cheeks almost as red as her flannel dressing-gown, and playing as if most truly her fate in this world depended on the disposal of the fated queen. And when the unfortunate lady fell finally to Uncle Charley's lot, the children's ecstasy of enjoyment knew no bounds.

12

"Teddy," said Babs, when Captain Conway
had gone to dress for dinner, "I promised
Uncle Charley that I'd be good, but how can I
tell that fings won't turn out naughty like the
letters did?"

"I don't know," answered her brother doubtfully.

"I wonder why it was so much naughtier to
be a postman than a p'liceman," continued the
little girl.   "It makes fings very puzzling!"

"What shall we pretend to be now?" asked
Teddy, who could not throw much light on the
subject.

"I'se tired of postmen," said Babs wearily.

"I think I'll pretend to be an engine-driver,"
Teddy decided after some deliberation.

"What's the goodest thing you know?"
asked Babs, anxious to make a safe choice this
time.

Teddy thought kings and queens, but Babs
hastened to remind him of the wicked kings
that Miss Grimston often read about in the
history lessons.

"Well, I don't know then."   Teddy gave it
up together with most other intricate problems.

"I know," cried Babs suddenly, "grown-up
soldiers what are officers.   Uncle Charley's an

officer himself, Father-in-Inja is an officer, and
Uncle Jack, and in course they are all verygood."

"So they are," agreed Teddy. "You'd
better be an officer, Babs."

"That'll be splendid and sure not to turn
out naughty," laughed Babs. "I are a real
officer, Teddy."

Babs soon got better again, though she did
not look quite so fat and brown, and she was
also rather graver and quieter than before.
Miss Grimston noted a marked improvement
in her behaviour in school-time, and there were
fewer scoldings and punishments even in the
strict atmosphere of the nursery. But it was
not altogether well with little Babs. A wistful look had quenched the merry sparkle of her
eyes and her mouth began to droop at the corners
which gave her rather a pitiful expression.

"Why don't you laugh and make things jolly
like you used to?" asked Teddy grumblingly,
one day when Babs was unusually quiet.

"I don't know," said the child sadly, "on'y I
are afraid fings will turn out naughty like they
did afore."

"Why do you bother about it?" asked her
brother.

"Oh, Teddy!" she exclaimed reproachfully,

" I can't help it, 'cause you see I promised Uncle Charley I'd be good."

Captain Conway himself was conscious of this change in Babs. He watched her keenly and closely and saw that she was no longer the bright, merry little creature he had found at Cloverdale only six months ago. And yet he felt unable to mend matters. His comfort was in the thought that her father and mother would now soon be home and the child restored, before it was too late, to the happy influences of home life in the country.

But nevertheless he could not be quite at ease about her, and in his helplessness he turned to his wife, but in vain.

" Can't you see what is wrong with the child?" he asked Aunt Eleanor almost pleadingly in his anxiety.

" I don't know what you mean," answered his wife carelessly. " I can see nothing."

" You won't see it," said Captain Conway irritably.

" For goodness' sake don't begin that all over again! I am perfectly sick of all this ridiculous fuss you make about Babs. And if she isn't quite so wild and noisy as she was, let us be thankfull."

"You don't understand," said Charley Conway impatiently, "and yet you ought to," he added sternly.

Eleanor Conway tossed her pretty head scornfully.

"I am not interested in nursery talk," she said in a hard voice. "If you want any more of it, you had better ring the bell for the nurse."

Her husband did not answer her. He was angry, but he was also suddenly conscious of a great mistake somewhere, which could never be set right ; and the pain of such a consciousness silenced all his hurrying words of irritation and displeasure.

Aunt Eleanor saw the strange look on his face, and she too knew that a crisis had come, though of its nature she was ignorant. But she did not mean to quarrel seriously. It was so silly to quarrel, and over such a trifle too as their little niece. Why need Charley bother so ? It was getting on his nerves, she thought. And he used to be so superior to nerves in his rackety, fast, steeple-chasing moods, which were Aunt Eleanor's standard of manliness.

And Uncle Charley, in his hunger for something he had missed, was thinking how hopeless it all was.

Yet Eleanor Conway was exactly the same woman as Eleanor West was when Charley Conway married her for her lovely face.

She was the first to break the pause.

" Ned and Barbara can't come home as they hoped, it is all uncertain whether Ned can get off now, and it may be years, Barbara says in to-day's letter."

" Aren't they coming in the spring, then ? " exclaimed Uncle Charley aghast.

" There seems no chance of it, and here we are saddled with these children interminably. Teddy of course can go to school, but Babs ! "

"Poor Babs!" said her uncle almost to himself as his wife went out of the room, "poor Babs!"

And then as Charley Conway sat thinking about it all, as he realised that his wife would not, and what was perhaps sadder still, could not, help him to do his duty to the child committed to his charge, a sudden big resolve burst into his heart—that Babs's life and character should not be thus spoiled by clumsy or cruel misunderstanding, and he himself would prevent it. That he would take the whole responsibility on his own shoulders, and carry it until he gave the child into her father and mother's care.

A very big resolve for Uncle Charley, who had lived entirely for self, and the passing amusements of the hour, shirking all work and responsibility as boring and burdensome.

But this new and nobler purpose filled up a little of the fresh-found emptiness of his life, and brought with it better and brighter days both for Uncle Charley and for Babs.

# CHAPTER X.

## CHRISTMAS.

" Is there Christmas in London same as there is in the country ? " asked Babs.

" Of course," answered Teddy loftily, " there is Christmas everywhere."

Babs's face brightened.

" I'se glad of that ! Then don't you fink, Teddy, we ought to be seeing to our money for presents ? "

" So we ought. Christmas comes in two weeks ; I heard nurse say so yesterday."

" I shall give Uncle Charley a splendid present," continued Babs enthusiastically, " the most splendidest that I can buy."

" Then you will have no money left for the others."

" There aren't no others," argued Babs, " no Nana, nor Giles, nor Mrs. Forrester."

" There's Aunt Eleanor, and Miss Grimston, and nurse."

" Oh, Teddy, I couldn't really give Miss

Grimston a Christmas present, 'cause we'll have a holiday on Christmas Day, and you couldn't give it on another day! And 'sides," added Babs truthfully, " I don't like her enough much."

" I will give Aunt Eleanor a little present," announced Teddy thoughtfully.

" I will give Uncle Charley an awful big one, and p'r'aps I will give nurse a needle-case what costs a penny."

" When shall we go shopping, Babs?"

" I'll ask Uncle Charley. He'll take us," added Babs, with a glad note of confidence in her voice. " What fun it will be!"

On the following morning Captain Conway heard a rapping at his dressing-room door at a very elementary stage of his toilet.

" You must wait a little longer," he shouted, for Babs's visits to her uncle's dressing-room had become quite an institution. They were among the new order of things that Uncle Charley had introduced into nursery administration, and were keenly appreciated by both children, especially Babs, who had often chafed behind the bars of the little wooden gate at the top of the stairs. But that detested barrier had been swept away, together with the command

that the children were not to come downstairs
unless sent for. They could always now be
sure of a welcome in any part of Uncle Charley's
domain.

" Don't we never bother you like we did
afore ? " asked Babs, amazed at this new dis-
pensation.

" No, little one," answered her uncle, half
smiling.

" We must have changed a good bit," said
Babs.

" Perhaps it is I who have changed ! " said
Uncle Charley.

And the children both laughed at anything
so utterly improbable.

" You see it is like this," began Babs, directly
the dressing-room door was unlocked, " we
want to buy some fings for Christmas, and we
fought you might see 'bout taking us out shopping one day."

" What made you think that ? " asked Uncle
Charley.

" Oh, 'cause you always see 'bout fings we
want," said Babs beaming all over, " and give
us fousands of treats."

So quickly do children forget the past in the
present.

"I DID IT!"

Uncle Charley looked pleased.

"What do you want to buy?" he asked.

"A needle-case for nurse—a penny one you know, and a fing for Teddy—a box of chocolates or a bicycle, or anything what he wants, and then the secret. I can't tell you what that is, 'cause it is just to you that it is a secret."

"Well, suppose we go directly after lunch to-day?" suggested her uncle smiling.

"S'pose we do!" laughed the child, clapping her hands. "How nice you always fink of fings!" she added fervently, stepping on to the edge of a sponge bath, which immediately stood upright, flooding the room with its contents.

It really was tiresome, such a mess all over everything. And the noise brought in Aunt Eleanor who was very angry indeed.

"I did it!" gasped Babs, to remove the erroneous impression that it had done it of itself.

"Then you are a very naughty child!" exclaimed her aunt.

Babs looked up at her uncle.

"It was an accident," said Captain Conway, gazing ruefully at his spotted shirts and soaked shoes.

"An accident climbing on to the edge of the bath! Nonsense!" interrupted Aunt Eleanor.

" Run upstairs and tell nurse to change your clothes," said Uncle Charley.

" Are I naughty or on'y an accident ? " asked the little girl anxiously.

She was somewhat in doubt as to whether Uncle Charley was angry as well as Aunt Eleanor.

" I don't think you are very naughty," said her uncle smiling.

Babs felt assured, and trotted off cheerfully upstairs, though she left rather loud, cross voices behind her.  Nurse, too, met her most disagreeably, and all during the process of redressing told her very stern stories of evil little girls who stood on the edges of sponge baths in which they were afterwards invariably drowned.

" Uncle Charley wasn't angry," said Babs in self-defence.

Nurse sniffed significantly.

" Why do you always smell so loud when I tell 'bout Uncle Charley ? " asked the child.

" Now then, none of your imperence ! " said nurse severely, giving Babs a harder shake than was necessary into her clean clothes.

" Perhaps Uncle Charley will whip you when you're dry," suggested Teddy calmly.

Babs stood still in the middle of a mouthful of bread and milk.

"Oh, Teddy!" she gasped, "I don't really fink so! He had not even a cross face, and not a bit a cross voice."

But still it was an unpleasant thought, and lay heavy on the child's soul as she went downstairs a little later, in answer to a summons Uncle Charley had sent up.

"I are dry now," she said gloomily, going up to his chair where he sat smoking, "kite dry enough to whip."

Her uncle laughed.

"But what made you think I was going to whip you?" he asked.

"Teddy fought so, and he made me fink it rather. Are you, Uncle Charley?" very anxiously.

Such a quaint concerned face, with round solemn eyes. Uncle Charley, stifling the temptation to increase its woe, kissed it back into brightness and laughter, and very dear to him was the earnest assurance :—

"I love you, Uncle Charley, much better'n anybody in the whole world!"

"Better than Giles?" asked Captain Conway.

" Oh, yes !   Better even than darling Soot ! "
she added in the height of fervent affection.

" And you won't ever stand on the edges of
baths again, will you ? " asked Uncle Charley
as an afterthought.

" Never no more, I promise ! " she answered
solemnly.

" You need not promise, little one, only try
to remember."

Wherein it was evident that Uncle Charley
had not watched thus carefully over his little
niece without learning something of the art of
managing her.

" An' will you take us shopping after all ? "
she asked a little wistfully.

" Of course I will ! " Uncle Charley assured
her.   And great was the delight of the nursery
world in consequence.

It was so important going off with their
purses in a hansom, and so exciting having a
whole shopful of splendid things to choose
from.

Babs buried her face in Uncle Charley's coat
while Teddy bought her present, and then
Teddy covered his face with his hat during
Babs's purchases.

" Now, Uncle Charley, you must be sure'n

not look while I buy the next fing," said Babs earnestly.

And Uncle Charley promised.

It was indeed dreadfully difficult to find something exactly suited to Babs's extraordinary taste. She was quite pale and exhausted with the mental strain when at last the parcel was done up, and Uncle Charley had returned from gazing out of the window to settle the pecuniary part of the transaction which was left over even after the children had emptied their purses on to the counter.

Just as they were leaving the shop Babs stopped.

" I want to whisper something," she said. And then as Uncle Charley stooped to listen : " I fink I will buy a little present for Aunt Eleanor, 'cause I would not like her to be at all 'pointed, you see, and she might be if there wasn't one at all from me."

" All right," said Uncle Charley with rather a sad smile, knowing how indifferent his wife would be in either case. " What shall we get ? "

" You choose ! "

But none of them took much interest in the purchase of a pretty little matchbox to go on Aunt Eleanor's silver table.

Babs was full of her parcel, concerning which
Uncle Charley made wildly improbable guesses,
and both children were intoxicated with the
mere atmosphere of a toy shop.

Altogether it was a delightful afternoon, but
it made the time between that and Christmas
seem terribly long.  So long that Babs thought
they must have skipped Christmas, as Teddy
always skipped the trade-winds in the geography lessons.   And downstairs a great argu-
ment was going on.   An invitation had come
for Uncle Charley and Aunt Eleanor to spend
Christmas at a house just out of London where
there was to be a dance on Christmas Eve, and
of course Aunt Eleanor meant to accept it.

But Uncle Charley upset everything by
declaring that he intended staying at home with
the children.

"How absurd you are!" exclaimed Aunt
Eleanor irritably; "why, it will be a lovely
dance, and a very jolly house-party!  The
Hartlands are going," she added, in the hope
that her husband would be persuaded by the
thought of meeting some great friends.

"I should like to go," said Captain Conway,
"only I will not disappoint the children."

"The children again!  Which means Babs

I presume ! " interrupted his wife disagreeably. And then as he made no answer she changed her tone.

" Do take me, Charley ! I want so dreadfully to go, and it will be an awful disappointment to me if you won't."

Uncle Charley was just going to refuse his wife's request when he remembered Babs's generosity :—

" I would not like her to be at all 'pointed, you see ". Baby consideration, but it influenced his decision and won Aunt Eleanor's cause.

" I will go for the dance, then," said Charley Conway slowly, " and we will come back to town on Christmas Day, and have the children down to late dinner, and a Christmas tree in the afternoon." With which Aunt Eleanor had to be content.

So Uncle Charley had a lovely Christmas tree made in secret ; and the children crept out of bed and hung up their stockings on Christmas Eve, after their usual happy custom.

Babs could not sleep very well for the excitement of Santa Claus and his nocturnal visit, so she jumped out of bed very early and felt for the enriched stocking. There it hung, hollow and limp as on the night before.

" Oh, Teddy ! " she almost groaned, stealing into his room, " Santa Claus has forgot."

" Forgot what ? " asked Teddy sleepily.

"Christmas !   And the stockings is kite empty ! " cried Babs in an anguish of disappointment.

The awful news banished sleep from Teddy's blue eyes, and the children sat together on the bed sorrowfully regarding the two empty black stockings with a woe almost too deep for words, till nurse came in with the unpleasant information that they were catching their deaths of cold.

Breakfast was very serious that morning, and Babs's bread-and-milk proved unusually choky.

The little girl sadly laid the needle-case on nurse's plate, and then nurse gave the children each a china mug with " Be good " stamped on in gold letters.

" Do you like the mugs, Teddy ? " asked Babs when they were alone together.

" No," answered her brother crossly, " I think they're horrid."

" I fink they will make drinking rather too scolding," continued Babs, " 'cause that big ' Be good ' 'minds me so much of nurse when she speaks scolding."

"You ought to remember people by their presents," said Teddy.

" I know! 'When this you see, remember me,' Mrs. Forrester always wrote in her presents. But I fink I'd rather forget nurse, wouldn't you, Teddy?"

" Yes, I would, and I hate her old presents!"

" Oh, Teddy, I fink it would be naughty and rather rude to hate them; but still I do wish that they hadn't been kite such stern mugs."

" Hullo, children! Where are you?" shouted Uncle Charley directly he came home. " A merry Christmas to you!"

"Oh! Uncle Charley!" screamed Babs, rushing into his arms, "we aren't a bit merry, 'cause Santa Claus kite forgot our stockings."

" What an idiot I am!" exclaimed Uncle Charley, who saw that his elaborate Christmas preparations had fallen so short of the mark; and then to the children :—

" It is all right, youngsters! Santa Claus left me his presents for a Christmas tree this afternoon; a splendid big jolly one," he added, smiling at the sudden change in their faces. " So we will have a merry Christmas after all!"

" Oh, yes," laughed Babs, " I'se so glad

you've come home, 'cause you make fings all
right again."

And it really was a beautiful tree, all covered
with tiny coloured candles and hung with the
loveliest presents ; just the very things the
children most wanted.

There was only one cloud.  Aunt Eleanor
gave Teddy and Babs a little tricycle between
them.  A very handsome present, but their aunt
did not know the anguish of a shared possession.

" Betweens aren't never nobody's real own,"
complained Babs afterwards ; and the very
wheels of that dainty little machine seemed
always weighed by the burdensome thought
that it was not the rider's very own.

"One's very own," is a mystic charm of
childhood that lends lustre even to a discarded
pen-wiper, or any treasure of the waste-paper
basket and rag-bag.

And when the tree was stripped of its
miscellaneous fruit, there was the excitement of
giving Uncle Charley his present.

" Guess once more afore you open it," said
Babs holding out the little parcel, soiled through
much handling.

Uncle Charley felt it carefully while the children shrieked with laughter.

"I guess an ink-pot," he said at last.

Babs clapped her hands.

"Now open it!" she screamed.

And there lay a big, wooden, tartan-painted *serviette* ring.

"Isn't it lovely!" exclaimed Babs proudly. "The plaid 'minded me so much of Giles's Sunday pocket-handkerchief. And it'll be so useful 'cause you can have it every day at lunch and dinner."

Uncle Charley kissed his thanks, and seemed so pleased that the children were delighted. And even Aunt Eleanor laughed a little too, and thanked Babs quite kindly for the matchbox.

"Here, Parker," said Captain Conway to the butler, "be sure and put this at my place at dinner to-night, and at lunch too."

"Oh, Charley!" interrupted Aunt Eleanor, as the children rushed off to superintend the laying of the table, "not at lunch to-morrow, the Hartlands are coming and it is too awfully vulgar."

"Yes, it is too awfully vulgar!" repeated her husband in a curious voice. He was not referring to Babs's taste in the wooden ring, but his wife's hopeless want of taste—in her incapability of ever seeing the deeper thing.

Once upon a time, and a very little while ago, Uncle Charley never looked for the deeper thing himself, and consequently never saw it. And as he was dressing for dinner that Christmas night he wondered how it was that things looked so different to him now, and then he caught Babs's earnest gaze.

" I suppose it is by seeing things through your eyes, little one," he said, smiling at her questioning face.

" I don't know what you are talking 'bout," answered Babs, laughing up at him.

But Uncle Charley knew what he was talking about. For to see the deeper thing we must look at life through other people's eyes. Which is sympathy.

# CHAPTER XI.

## FATHER-AND-MOTHER-IN-INJA.

Now the question was whether Father-and-Mother-in-Inja were to become Father-and-Mother-in-England at all during Babs and Teddy's childhood.

Major and Mrs. Conway were very much puzzled about it out in India, and Uncle Charley and Aunt Eleanor were very anxious in England, but the children themselves never gave it a thought. The memory even of Nana was growing faint, and the misty hopes of a good father and mother were entirely swallowed up in the glad reality of a kind uncle.

"There's on'y one fing I would like," said Babs, "I would like us and Uncle Charley to live at Cloverdale with Giles for our nurse, and Aunt Eleanor and real nurse to stay in London for ever and ever."

But Teddy had begun to go to school, and he greatly enjoyed the companionship of other boys, and above all the games in Kensington

Gardens in the middle of the day, which one of the younger masters organised.

This was rather a sore point with Babs, because Teddy never would acknowledge her in any way if she met the school out walking, and it cut poor Babs to the quick.

"It's silly to nod to you," argued Teddy; "the other boys don't, and they would laugh at me."

"But I'm not their sisters," said Babs meekly.

"Other fellows don't meet their sisters, and I don't like to meet mine," said Teddy, who was an English schoolboy fledged on the first day of the term.

"P'r'aps they haven't got no sisters," muttered Babs, who was terribly ashamed of being in such a humiliating position of relationship.

Teddy's going to school made it very dull for Babs, and Uncle Charley interfered.

"I won't have her shut up alone with that old Grimston ogre," he said to Aunt Eleanor. "You must get a young, jolly governess."

"I don't know the kind you want, so you had better interview them yourself," witheringly.

And this was Aunt Eleanor's revenge.

Female after female arrived in answer to the

advertisement, and Uncle Charley bravely saw them all. The process he felt aged him con-siderably, but, thanks to his selection, red-cheeked, merry Miss Drew now reigned in the schoolroom, and lessons became games under kindergarten administration, while playtime was truly a dream of delight.

For Maggie Drew had half a child's heart even in her twenty-fifth year, and she was in touch with many little brothers and sisters in the nursery at home, and with all other children for their sakes.

Uncle Charley peeped into the schoolroom one morning and found Babs and her new governess enveloped in huge pinafores making clay models of all kinds of quaint animals. A lovely kind of play-work which taught Babs more natural history in an hour than all Miss Grimston's *Pleasant Pages* put together.

"Your pig is too thin. Fatten it up, or mine will be ready for killing first," he heard Miss Drew say, and then peals of laughter followed him as he went downstairs.

"She is the right sort at last," he thought thankfully as he lit his cigarette.

"Please may I have another help of lemon sponge?" asked Babs at luncheon.

"Certainly not," said Aunt Eleanor, "you have had two already."

"But I'm very hungry," pleaded Babs, as if lemon sponge were the most substantial of viands.

"You are very greedy, Babs," continued her aunt.

"No, I aren't, on'y lemon sponge is so very melting afore you can bite it. The last help I had was nothing but warm air."

Uncle Charley laughed.

"I don't believe you are really a greedy little girl," he said kindly, "but I have a thought."

"Oh, I loves your foughts!" interrupted Babs.

"I will buy you a bottle of sweets for your very own and it shall be kept in the sideboard cupboard, and you can have one whenever you like without asking. Only you must use your right judgment about it, and then you can show us that you are not greedy."

"Oh, Charley, how ridiculous!" said Aunt Eleanor. "The child will be ill in no time."

"I'm not so sure of that," said her husband. "People of five years old should learn to use their sense."

And when he came in that night he brought a lovely big bottle of acid drops, and Babs thought the one he gave her to taste was " kite the most 'licious sweet I ever eated ".

For two or three days Babs was very careful.

" It makes it so splendid and exciting not having to ask leave every time," she told Teddy.

" I'se going to have a sweet," announced the little girl just as lunch was over a few days afterwards, and she climbed down off her chair.

Aunt Eleanor shrugged her shoulders, and Uncle Charley observed : " I don't think I should eat a sweet directly after a big dinner if I were you, but of course you can if you like".

" It's my right judge !" said Babs, flushing up and tossing her head.

" All right," said Uncle Charley.

But Babs was a long time at the cupboard door.

" What are you doing with your pinafore ? " asked her aunt suddenly.

" I'se wiping my acid drop dry," exclaimed Babs, " 'cause I don't fink I'll eat a sweet 'rectly after a big dinner, and if I put it back in the bottle afore it's dry it'll stick to the others."

Uncle Charley and Aunt Eleanor both

laughed, and her uncle stooped to kiss Babs
before he went out.

" You are not a greedy little girl I see," he
said gently.

" I knewed I wasn't, on'y I had rather a narrow 'scape to-day, didn't I, Uncle Charley ? "
she added solemnly.

The next mail from India brought very good
news for Babs and Teddy.

Father-and-Mother-in-Inja were really coming
home after all, coming almost at once with
Nana and the baby sister, to fetch the children
from London and take them home again to dear
old Cloverdale.

When Uncle Charley told them, Teddy and
Babs were full of delight and excitement for
quite ten minutes. They were at schoolroom
tea, which meal was generally enlivened by
Teddy's thrilling accounts of the perils and
penalties of school life. From which it would
appear that he was one of the most dare-devil
characters that had ever defied school discipline,
though in reality little Conway was a model of
timid propriety in the actual awe-inspiring
presence of the masters.

" Will Father-and-Mother-in-Inja take me
away from school ? " asked Teddy anxiously.

"Will they take me away from you, dear Uncle Charley?" questioned Babs.

"They will arrive just in time for the holidays, and take you back to spend them at Cloverdale."

"You too?" persisted Babs, holding fast his coat sleeve.

"Perhaps," said Uncle Charley, with a tender look in his eyes.

"I wants to show you the new chair in my dolls' house, what Miss Drew taught me to make. Will you 'scuse me?" she asked the governess, who gave a smiling consent.

But Uncle Charley was horrified to see a decaying bit of cheese reposing on the grand new chair. He instantly seized it and threw it in the fire.

"Oh!" screamed Babs, "you have killed the little darlings! Why did you?" in an agony of reproach.

"It was a nasty bit of cheese and smelt horribly," exclaimed Uncle Charley amazed.

"But it was our pet mites!" said Babs sadly, "and now they is all burned kite dead."

"Never mind, little one! They are not nice pets for you to have. And you will soon have all your splendid country pets again."

"Oh, yes!" cried Babs, quickly diverted. "I do wonder how many of darling Soot's kittens will be alive, and if the rabbits are kite well."

So the interest of their parents' coming centred in the thought of Cloverdale, and Father-and-Mother-in-Inja were regarded as the passports to that enchanted home.

One night Babs had been fast asleep for quite two hours when a murmuring of voices disturbed her and she slowly opened her big brown eyes to see a most surprising sight.

A strange lady was leaning over her bed, and by the fireplace sat Nana with a crumpled bundle of white draperies on her knee.

"Oh, Nana!" shrieked Babs directly her sleepy brain decided that it was not all a dream, and the little girl flew out of bed, brushing past the strange lady, straight into Nana's disengaged arm.

"There, Miss Babs, darling," said Nana, after a very big hug; "now go and kiss your mamma."

The strange lady was standing alone by the empty bed, gazing at Babs with hungry eyes.

"Come, my darling," she said in rather a broken voice. For somehow Barbara Conway

had never realised before that her home-coming would be nothing to her little daughter compared with Nana's—that she was only a stranger while the nurse was a dearly-loved friend.

Babs stood still with wondering eyes.

" She is a bit sleepy, ma'am," explained Nana.

" No, I aren't," interrupted Babs gravely, " I are finking 'bout fings."

" Oh, Babs ! " cried the lady, " won't you come to me ?  I am your mother, you know."

" The mother out of Father-and-Mother-in Inja ? " asked Babs drawing nearer.

" Yes, darling," very gently.

" Then I will kiss you," said Babs, holding up her face, " and where is the other one ? "

" Here he is ! " cried Uncle Charley, who was standing in the doorway with his brother. " And this is Babs," he added proudly, as the child rushed into his arms and he lifted her up to kiss her father.

" You is like Uncle Charley," said Babs, looking into Major Conway's face critically, " I'se glad of that."

" We're brothers you know," answered her father.

" And are you as nice as him ? " Babs asked
a little anxiously.

" Nicer," said Uncle Charley, and then they
all laughed.

Barbara Conway looked rather sadly at the
merry group, she seemed so outside her little
daughter's world, and she did not know that
Babs's experience led the child to shrink from
grown-up ladies like Aunt Eleanor.

But Uncle Charley, seeing the same wistful
look in his sister-in-law's brown eyes that he
had tried so hard to banish from her little
daughter's, understood, and held out the child
to her mother.

" There, Babs," he said gently, " you will
be the happiest little girl in the whole world
now Father-and-Mother-in-Inja have come to
take care of you in England. Give your
mother a very big kiss, because she loves you
so much and has wanted you all these years
so dreadfully."

" And do you want me now ? " Babs asked,
holding her mother's face in her two fat hands,
and gazing into it earnestly.

" Yes, my darling, much more than I can tell
you." And Barbara Conway felt as if she
must break down.

" Then I'se glad you've come, and I will love you too, and kiss you tight and hard like I do Uncle Charley," promised Babs. And her mother stayed with her whispering very tender, soothing talk till Babs's sleepy eyes closed. And when Ned Conway came up to look for his wife he found her with her head on Babs's pillow, and his little daughter's rosy cheek pressed close against her mother's.

The next morning Babs rushed into Teddy's room, feeling very superior.

" Did you see Father-and-Mother-in-Inja last night ? " she asked, hoping most fervently that he had not.

" No," said Teddy ; " I never woke in the night at all."

" I did," exclaimed Babs proudly, " and I know them now kite well. Father 'minds me very much of Uncle Charley, but Mother isn't a bit like Aunt Eleanor."

Teddy jumped into his clothes as quickly as time and cold fingers would permit, and he and Babs tore downstairs. A tall gentleman ran out and caught them on the second landing, and before breakfast Teddy knew Father-and-Mother-in-Inja almost as well as Babs did.

"Can you play cricket?" Teddy asked his father at breakfast.

"Rather!" exclaimed Uncle Charley, "why your father is a splendid cricketer, old fellow!"

"And you shall be one too, my boy," said Major Conway, "we will practise all the holidays."

And with a father who was a first-class cricketer, what more could any English schoolboy want?

"Mother," said Babs afterwards, jumping on to her knee violently, and putting one fat arm as far as it would reach round Mrs. Conway's neck, "do you mind much 'bout me not being pretty like Aunt Eleanor does?"

"Oh, my darling! What do you mean? I think you are the dearest, nicest little daughter in the whole world, and I would not have you one tiny bit different."

"Wouldn't you?" exclaimed Babs amazed. "Hadn't you rather my hair was golden or something?"

"No, no!" her mother assured her. "I love you best just as you are, dear."

"I'se so glad," murmured the child, "'cause it makes there nothing nasty to fink about."

Just then Nana came in with the baby.

" My new sister is very funny," observed Babs, regarding her with interest, " but I don't fink she will ever be able to walk, Mother, do you ?   Her feet are 'zactly like moles' feet."

" They are not quite big and strong enough yet, but very soon baby will run about and play with you."

" And make up for Teddy's being at school. Oh, Mother, I are glad you came, 'cause it was so dull afore when Teddy went to school ! "

" It won't be dull ever again, for we shall be at Cloverdale, and you will have baby and me always to play with."

" Can you play ?   I didn't fink grown-up ladies ever could play.   I fought it messed their dresses."

" Mine don't matter, and we will wear comfortable old ones."

" That'll be jolly ! " laughed Babs.   " And, Mother, we will take Uncle Charley to Cloverdale, too ? "

"Oh, yes, your father and Uncle Charley used to play together when they were little boys, and they will want to play together again now."

" Me too.   Uncle Charley's sure to let me play with them.   He always does, you see, Mother."

"You are very fond of Uncle Charley, I think, Babs."

"In course I am.   I b'long to Uncle Charley, you know."

"Not to your father and me ?" exclaimed her mother.

Babs looked puzzled.

"Half to you and half to Father, but I fink the biggest half to Uncle Charley."

"Yes, dear, that is it, you belong to us because we are your father and mother, but I think you must always belong to Uncle Charley too, because he has been so good to you."

"I don't fink we will take Aunt Eleanor to Cloverdale," added Babs, and just then the baby began to cry, which changed the conversation.

But her mother heard and understood.

# CHAPTER XII.

## HOME AGAIN.

" DADDY, Daddy ! " shouted Babs, scrambling
through the morning-room window at Cloverdale
and tearing across the lawn.

" Here I am, what is it ? " called Major Conway from the cricket pitch where he and Teddy
were having a little practice.

" Have you seen Dash ?   Mummy and me's
lost him and we'se rather 'fraid 'bout the new
chickens."

"No; he hasn't come this way," said her father,
stooping to kiss the dear, brown little face, which
looked up so eagerly into his own.   He could
not help kissing Babs whenever he met her, she
had such splendid fat cheeks and such a merry,
laughing face altogether that it was irresistible.

How the children did love being back at
Cloverdale ; and it was far nicer now than ever
before because Father-and-Mother-at-home were
so much better and dearer and jollier than
Father-and-Mother-in-Inja !

Every single day was so happy, unspoiled by
the curse of best frocks, or gloves, or even
continual cleanliness.    And Babs was almost
intoxicated with the bliss of those long summer days after her year of life in London.

" Dash hasn't come this way, Mummy,"
called Babs as Mrs. Conway appeared in the
distance, and then she started running towards
her mother with all the speed of which her
short fat legs were capable.

" Then we must go and look for him in the
poultry-yard ; I'm afraid he has gone there."

" I'se 'fraid so, too."

And their fear was fully realised, for at the
very entrance to the poultry-yard lay a beautiful big chicken quite dead, while Dash, with the
innocent countenance dogs know so well how
to assume, sat gazing at the beauties of Nature,
evincing a slightly bored interest in the question as to how the best white chicken could
possibly have met with its death.

" Oh, Mummy ! " gasped Babs, gazing with
sorrow on the murdered fowl ; " and it looked
as if it was just going to lay a little boiled
egg."

" Never mind, darling !   But it is really very
naughty of Dash."

Babs promptly made for the degenerate spaniel, but Dash had apparently just remembered an important engagement at the other end of the garden and hastened to fulfil it.

" Is anybody coming to lunch to-day ?" asked Babs presently.

" Yes ; a soldier friend of Daddy's."

" Soldiers aren't kite what I used to fink when I was little, Mummy."

"Aren't they, dear ? Why not ? "

" Well, you see, they kill fewer people, and play games a good lot more than fighting. I know heaps of soldiers now. Uncle Charley, and Daddy, and Uncle Jack, and the friend what is coming to-day makes four."

" But then you don't see them in battles, you know, Babs."

" No," said the child doubtfully. " But, Mummy, I fink it's nicer to play games than kill people, and I are glad that Uncle Charley and Daddy is that sort."

Her mother laughed.

" I think Daddy and Uncle Charley are the right sort, too."

" The very rightest in the whole world ! " said Babs enthusiastically.

" This is my little girl," said Major Conway,

introducing Babs to his friend just before luncheon.

"And how many of you are there?" Captain Eardley asked her presently.

"Three, and the paroquet makes four," answered Babs quickly. "And Teddy goes to school, but I have a governess. I can do lots of sums," she added proudly, "adding and taking-away ones."

"That is very clever of you," said the gentleman.

"It is not kite so clever as it might be," she confessed candidly, "'cause the last little girl what my governess taught could do borrowing afore she was six. But though I are rather backward in my lessons I are very forward in my play, Teddy says."

After lunch Mrs. Conway and the children went out into the garden, and Teddy induced his mother to bowl to him for a little, but Babs for some occult reason returned to the dining-room where the gentlemen were smoking.

"Run away now, Babs," said her father.

"Daddy, I'se 'fraid I can't," answered the child, with a flushed face but fixed expression.

Major Conway was intensely surprised. "Babs!" he exclaimed. "What do you mean?"

"I feels I must stay," continued Babs, "'cause I want to so dreadful much."

Her father did not care to prolong the contest, or bore his friend with domestic discipline, so he proposed a game of billiards, and the gentlemen walked off, leaving Babs standing in the middle of the room with crimson cheeks.

"I am sorry you are a disobedient little girl," Major Conway said gravely as he went out and shut the door.

After a few minutes' deliberation Babs walked slowly down to the cricket pitch, and stood looking on with so solemn a face that her mother's attention was attracted.

"Has anything gone wrong, Babs?" she asked quickly.

"Something has gone wrong," answered Babs impressively.

"What is it, dear?"

Babs looked bored.

"I fink it is too difficult to tell you, Mummy!"

"Oh, no, my darling, come and sit on my knee and whisper it."

"I fink I could tell it better from here," said Babs, looking straight up into the sky.

"Very well, dear. What is it?"

Babs continued gazing heavenwards and observed :—

" I are naughty ".

" What kind of naughtiness ? " asked her mother surprised.

" The worst what there is," replied Babs, with such earnestness as befitted so serious a confession.

Mrs. Conway stifled a strong desire to laugh.

" And what is that ?   Tell me all about it."

" Disobedience to Daddy," continued Babs, becoming interested in the narrative, " and he is very sorry 'bout it.   Not a nice comforting kind of sorry, but rather a stern, solemn sorry."

" Oh, Babs !   And I hope you are sorry, too."

" I fink I shall be soon," said Babs discreetly ; " but I can't be kite sure yet."

" Well, dear, directly you are sure I would go and tell Daddy, if I were you."

" It rained yesterday when I was out," began Babs irrelevantly, " very hard drops of rain."

And then she picked up her hat and walked slowly away, swinging it by the elastic and talking aloud to herself to keep up her spirits.

" It is very hot to-day, and rather uncomfort-

able, too. I 'spects that's what makes my
cheeks so thirsty. I will go and dig in my
garden, and then I shall be kite happy."

But digging in her garden even did not make
Babs happy.

" It keeps getting uncomfortabler," she continued, stopping to rest, "and my old fings
aren't growing a bit nice," giving some precious
radish tops a vicious smack with her spade.
" P'r'aps they want water. It'll be jolly watering them with my watering-can."

But somehow even the watering-can failed to
charm.

" The water seems wetter than it gener'ly is,"
she said crossly, stooping down to rub a big
splash off her stocking, and then she kicked
the can right over, and stood gloomily watching
the wandering streams of water on the path.

" Sakes alive!" observed Giles, coming up
at that moment, "what a mess the child be
making to be sure! What's the matter, little
missy?" he asked, seeing her disconsolate
face.

" Nothing is the matter, Giles," said Babs,
drawing herself up, "and I fink you are very
interfering to call my garden ' what a mess '."

Old Giles looked at Babs in amazement.

" My conscience alive ! " he observed.    " You
are in the tantrums to be sure and no mistake."

Babs flushed up to the roots of her hair.

" When people are very hot and uncomfortable, Giles," she explained, " and other people

HOME AGAIN.

will keep on talking so much it makes it very —
very "—racking her brains for a suitable epi-
thet—" very beastly indeed. My garden wanted
watering badly, and in course I was 'bliged to
'tend to it."

And Babs marched away, trying to look as dignified as a fat little girl in a dirty pinafore can.

She went across the orchard and down the steps round the corner right on to the lower lawn, where Major Conway was sitting alone in the shade.

" Oh ! " exclaimed Babs in surprise, and then stood still.

" Babs ! " called her father, " come here to me ! "

Babs advanced slowly. She was a little in doubt as to how events would shape themselves.

" Babs," said Major Conway very gravely, " have you anything to say to me ? "

Babs looked up to the sky and down to the ground.

" I have something, but it is almost too hard to say now. I fought it might be easier after tea."

" It will be harder after tea. Try to say it now, little one."

" Oh, you speaked just like Uncle Charley, then ! " exclaimed Babs, brightening a little ; " and I are sorry I was naughty, Daddy."

" That is right," said her father, lifting her on to his knee and kissing her.

" Now I are sorry will you leave off being ? "

" Yes, Babs. And you will not be disobedient any more, will you ? "

" No, I won't. And do you know I fink it
was you being sorry and me not what made
fings all so hot and uncomfortable ? "

" Yes, that was it."

" Well, I'se good now, Daddy, kite good.
Oh, here's Mummy come ! Mummy ! " she
shouted at the top of her voice, " I have left
off being naughty, and Daddy has kite for-
gived me."

" That's all right ! " cried Mrs. Conway,
and as she came up to him : " I shall soon be
quite a cricketer ; even Teddy says I am
improving in my bowling."

" We must have a match," said Major Conway.

" Oh, yes," cried Babs, " you and I will
play Mummy and Teddy." And then as her
brother scoffed at such a girlish idea : " Daddy,
I want to ask you something. Will you give
me some little-onias for my garden ? "

" Some little what ? "

" Onias. You have big-onias in your garden, and I fought I would like some little ones
in mine."

Her father and mother both laughed. "Your garden looks rather sloppy," said Major Conway regarding the damp plot.

"That's the naughtiness," remarked Babs truthfully, "it made me rather over-water it, I fink."

"That was a pity," said the major.

"It was!" echoed Babs solemnly.

There was great excitement at Cloverdale when Major Conway's big packing-cases arrived from India. The relics of his sport there excited the children beyond all bounds, and inspired Babs with most Oriental pretences. The garden became a jungle and every day full of thrilling adventures with tigers, elephants or bears. She never went out without her little toy gun as a protection against these savage beasts, and Major Conway was called upon to tell endless stories of the adventures he had met with in his life of sport in India.

"I have shot free tigers this morning," announced Babs one day at luncheon, "an' two of them was man-eaters."

"You had good sport then?" said her mother, who always entered splendidly into the children's pretences.

"I had!"

"What shall you do with the skins?" asked Major Conway.

"I shall send them to the Brickish Museum, Daddy. My Indian servants is getting them kite ready now."

"That is all right. And did you see any other animals?"

"I did! I saw a black panther creeping round the tool-house, and four hyenas in the wood, 'sides a wild boar and a grey ape."

Babs's imagination had always been active, but fed by her father's stories and her own recently acquired power of reading to herself, it grew much more luxuriantly. But Teddy's was fading fast, swamped by the glorious reality of cricket and the English boy's passion for games. Besides he was a schoolboy now, and was quickly becoming the heartless, mindless, soulless creature which is generally to be found in preparatory and public schools; but he was a healthy, happy little fellow notwithstanding, and his father rejoiced in his good length bowling and steady batting, which after all are so much more suited to schoolboy life and ambition than a thoughtful temperament or a vivid imagination. His mother laughed lovingly at his boyish brag, and even consented, at his earnest request, to allow the barber to cut the curling ends off his golden hair. So Teddy ceased to be a child and became a boy.

" I'se been reading to myself," said Babs, " and it was 'bout a very sad thing."

" What was it, darling? " asked Mrs. Conway. Babs seized upon any and every book she could find, and her parents loved to listen to her literary experiences.

" It was 'bout a very good lady what was a martyr. What is a martyr, Mummy? " Then without waiting for an answer :—"And she was eat by lions in the Empi-affeter."

" How dreadful ! " exclaimed Mrs. Conway.

" Why are you laughing, Daddy? 'cause it really was kite a solemn, sad story."

" Do you like sad stories ? " her father asked her hurriedly.

" I like all the stories what was ever written," replied Babs enthusiastically.

" I don't," said Teddy, " 'cause books are a sort of lessons, and lessons are all a fag."

" You like games best, my son," said his mother smiling.

" Rather ! " exclaimed Teddy, " and cricket best of all. Don't you ? "

" Well, since I hurt my hand so much trying

to catch that ball of Daddy's, I am not so fond
of cricket.   For to tell the truth I am frightened of those fast balls."

"Which are you most frightened of, Mummy?" asked Babs, whose mind was still in the
jungle; "fast balls or black panthers?"

"Fast balls just now, dear."

"And I am.   Teddy calls me butter-fingers,
but I really can't catch them 'cause they're so
full of hurting."

"That's just like a girl!" exclaimed Teddy
scornfully, "you are such a coward!"

"Oh, Teddy! I'm not.   You have to be kite
as brave to kill and hunt wild beasts as to catch
quick balls."

"But you don't kill wild beasts," exclaimed
Teddy, "that's only pretending."   Babs stood
aghast at this heresy.

"I shouldn't be at all 'prised if you was to
be eaten by that pack of wolves what I saw in
the plantation this morning," she said loftily.

"Stuff   and   rubbish!"   answered Teddy
rudely.

"Babs, Babs!" called her mother, "here is
a letter for you from Uncle Charley."

"Oh, how splendid!   But, Mummy, I do
wish Uncle Charley would come here soon

'stead of writing. Uncle Charley and me miss each other very bad."

" Yes, dear, I know."

But neither Mrs. Conway nor any one else knew how much the captain missed his little niece.

Babs left an empty room in the house in Onslow Square, but Aunt Eleanor soon filled that with smart clothes and new dresses, and was glad of the space. And Babs also left an empty room in Uncle Charley's life. A room which could not be filled by race-horses, or polo-ponies, or club friends, or any of the gaieties of former London seasons. A quiet, dark room wherein lay a few dusty toys and baby memories, yet Uncle Charley chose to live in it rather than in the glaring, gas-lit atmosphere which was Aunt Eleanor's native air. And as he waited alone in this empty room, Charley Conway's eyes grew accustomed to the darkness, and he saw for the first time in his life, as the legacy that Babs had unconsciously left him, the outline of the Ideal.